Who is not afraid of the lunatics?

Mehdi Rezaei

Title: Who is not afraid of the lunatics?
Writer: Mehdi Rezaei
Translator: Ibrahim Daryaei Motlagh
Publisher: Supreme Century, Reseda, CA, USA
ISBN: 978-1939123497
Library Congress Control Number: 2018915111

Mehdi Rezaei is writer, researcher and instructor of story writing. He was born May 20th 1983 ans lives in Tehran.

Yet, 5 works of him have been published and he's doing research and instructs story telling for about 7 years. The main theme of his works is critical-social and he uses different kinds of story telling methods. His works have been translated to Kurdish, Swedish, Russian and English.

He is also chief of electronic magazine named "Chook", of which has been published 100 numbers monthly up to now.

He is also chief of global day of translation and story telling in Iran congress.

I want to show you the scenes that touch you like a slap in the face, put your safety in danger and blemish it. You may as well avoid watching them, you might turn them off and hide your identity, as murderers do, but you will not be able to stop the truth. No one will be able to.

Kaveh Golestan

Iranian photographer

Who is not afraid of the lunatics?

Everyone is insane. Only their insanity differs. These words are more than enough to let the others guess how insane I am. Others are often afraid that they might be called insane but, I am not afraid at all. I even enjoy my insanity. I write it on paper and put my signature below it, if I feel the need to do so. I am also bold enough to stare at others and call them insane when I see they do not talk and behave like sane people.

I am too willing to hear them to blow a fuse and beat the hell out of them. Once, I quarreled with a tramp on the subway. She was talking loudly on her cell phone telling her client how much money she wanted to sleep with him for one night. I got mad and we had a row. She swore at me, but I said nothing until she was about to get off, then I ripped her dress apart up to her neck from behind. By the time she wanted to do something, it was too late, the door had closed, and I gave her the middle finger.

These days, Negar is the only person who dares to call me insane. She says that my insanity is the type that picks on others; she says there is nothing that

I haven't picked on yet: The Lord, the Heaven, the earth, the people. One day that we had a row, Negar shouted: "You're insane! My dad and brother don't know anything about politics and literature and you keep arguing to outsmart them."

"Well, if they know so little about something, they should not bring it up." I said.

She looked into my eyes, and while she was in a crying mood, she said: "You're so stupid. Is there anything that you haven't messed with so far?"

Of course, what she said is very much true but certainly unfair. I don't argue with her about her work, her cooking, and her way of talking, but she feels comfortable to nagging me about watching films, and having arguments. So far she has put up with my insanity for about a year, yet I feel worried that one of these days she might just say that she cannot stand it any longer.

I have returned from school and am watching a film that I have already seen eight times. Anytime Negar is about to say something, I say: "Shhh! This is when it gets interesting".

Unlike many people, I don't get offended if they say I am insane right to my face. Because I just know that if I and the others like me, haven't been caged yet, it is because we haven't revealed the truth and honesty of our insanity. Take me for an example: I comb my hair back; I let a goatee grow on my chin and the side of my face cleanly shaved; I wear a suit and I hold a Papco case; I go to school and I teach from the morning to the evening.

This ordinary appearance makes other think I am insane. But I mentioned I don't get offended if I am called insane. So, perhaps, it would be better not to dress well, not to speak so elegantly, or have a goatee. Perhaps, it is better to stare into people's eyes like homeless and dirty tramps so that they can call me insane. Or I could write what I am writing now and have it published so that my wish could come true and the friends in the neighborhood would come around, and with one voice, call me "insane!" "insane!".

-Arman, why are you laughing like that?

-Me? I'm just watching a film.

-What's so funny in the film, "*The Unfaithful?*". Is 'a woman cheating on her husband' funny to you?

-Shhh! This is where it gets interesting.

She just stares at me silently. She wants to stop me by acting like this, but I am too cheeky and bold to mind the look she gives me. I remember that I have something to do, so I get up.

-I am going to see Mr. Shahi.

She continues to give me the look. I say: "I promise; I will be back soon. I don't know what he wants from me. It must be important, I guess. I'll be back soon"

- "I don't understand what you're doing with that robot that you haven't told me."

- "The poor thing is so lonely. I have told him that I will keep him company so he won't get depressed from loneliness."

- "I wish you had the same feeling about me too; I am getting fed up with what you do." She opens her weblog and reads her new post.

"This life is generally so worthless and it is not worth talking about. But I guess two things give it some value: belief in god and love. Often when we hear anything about them, we want to sick up. I am sure there are who, think that life is worthless without them, but they have been so belittled in our minds that they see our whole existence as only a dumping. Who or what killed the idea of god and love in us? Let us remember not to let anyone belittle God in our eyes, remember when we make fun of love, we are actually making fun of ourselves. Why shouldn't there be any hedge round the concepts of our existence? Why should we let someone rob our minds of the good ideas and leave other useless things in their place?"

All the big happenings spring from our small and unfenced minds; to know God and love, one must know where to go and who to ask. Many have sought god only to fall into their own hell. Many have looked for love only to feel hatred.

We were born into the world, whether we like it or not, Into this worthless world. But we must keep in mind that our belief is what good this existence value. Six decades have passed since my birth. Maybe I have grasped this important point too late, but it doesn't matter. It only matters that I have grasped it after all…

And he continues: "Now wait, I'll read the opinions for you."

I nod and say: "I am listening."

But in my heart I say: "Damn you, I can read all of them at my home. Do you really have to drag me to your house and put that thing on your throat and start scraping my brain?"

The first comment: If you think this life is worthless, that's your idea. I don't share such an idea. It is you who are worthless with these pseudo-philosophical and nonsensical ideas of yours. Good luck.

The second comment: I agree with the first sentence and disagree with the rest of it. What is God? What does love mean?

The third comment: I don't believe in God. If there is a God, then where is he while his people tear each other apart like cats and dogs? If there is one, then he has created us to watch us get killed. What is good about such a god?

The fourth comment: Love? You'd better write about hatred.

The fifth comment: May god cure you. Amen!

The sixth comment: I have read yet another interesting writing from you. I am glad to know that you still have a fresh breath. You put a good idea in my head, which is to defend my mental concepts and have a hedge for myself. Keep in touch with me too. I'm updated.

The seventh comment: This life is worthless and so are you and so am I. This whole life has no value and nothing can give it any value either.

The eighth comment: A friend said that god is a child that has an ant farm. Do you know what I am saying?

The ninth comment: We can say many things about what you said. Be online at 11 o'clock so we can chat.

He wants to read the tenth comment and the ones after it. I loudly sigh to show him that I am exhausted. He realizes that I'm tired. While I always try to have respect for him, had he not realized it, I could have turned back and said, "you idiot! Stupid! Dummy! I'm tired and I have a life to attend to". I always use these three words when I swear. After all, I am a literature teacher and I should not use taboo words. I don't use the dirty swear words like those I hear from the stupid people that don't have a cow's intelligence.

- "I know you are tired Mr. Teacher. We can leave the rest of it for some other time. But it is quite interesting that I still go on living hopefully, though I have lost my son in the war and my wife in an accident. My white hair and this old and wrinkled face still owns a happy spirit. Still, I fight for humanity and values. I despise people who do not grasp the concept of god and love. I wish this world could become awash like the time of Noah. Of course, it is not unlikely: The ice from the poles are melting; The islands are disappearing; Our turn will come too."

- "By the way, why did God soak the earth?" He felt shame. "For what?"

- "For creating humankind", he explains. "When misery had filled the earth, God thought that it was better for the world to have a fresh start. Those few faithful men and women were enough for the new world. If there is still a world, the credit must go to the faithful believers."

-I am not believing it because humans are now more miserable and corrupt than they were in the past. If it was god reason everything had to be under the water now.

-I told you not to hurry. One day, water will cover the earth again. And if it won't, people will drown in their own shit.

I say nothing, then he asks.

- "Do you know why I love you?"

- "No."

- "Because you don't care about me and my ideas. You don't try to impose what you know and believe. I don't try to force my ideas for anyone either; I just like to talk about them. That's it."

The truth is I don't give a damn what idea he has. He is also sick with this kind of insanity; the insanity of humanity and values. He thinks that by writing weblogs, he is taking a huge step in the path of humanity. I say: "well, let him enjoy his craziness too. Why bother to argue about it? Where did we get the few times that we did argue" when we first met?

I like some of his writing and I dislike the others. I am unlucky to be his confidante to meet him in his house once a week to hear the things on his weblog. He says: "I know that you can visit my weblog at home but I need someone to talk to".

As far as can tell, his whole life is the internet. He keeps surfing the net and weblogs chatting with others about political and philosophical issues. Of course, I am also interested in mingling with him. I like trying to make sense of his lif;. I like him talking about the whole of his life. But he rarely does that. He does not say anything directly about these things. So, I have no choice other than speaking with him to get gist of it.

2

Hello. I have been familiar with your magazine for a good while. I am so glad. Because I can now write to you about my past while I have never had the chance to tell anyone about it. You know, a couple of years ago, something happened in my life and I thought it was better to write it for you so that you can publish it, in case any girls like me had the same problem, they can got through it to determine their destiny with a little courage.

I say: Oh, so this is one those types who think their life events are so important that everyone must know them?

Negar says: Arman, don't be funny for God's sake. This letter is different from the others. For God's sake, just listen.

I am a murderer. Don't be too hasty to judge. I just want to tell you that I was so happy with this murder that I liked to soak in his dirty blood. I am not a hired assassin. I am no murderer, no lunatic or insane person. I just know that I killed him in defending my reputation and honor. Sometimes I say to myself I shouldn't have done so but again I say I did it because I had to. Because I had no other way. The problem with Mastaneh, Leila, Shila, and

Mitra was annoying me like fleas and so I murdered him. No, I don't want to accuse anyone else of this murder. I did it because I felt with my whole heart that I had to do it. Now, I can only say that my life is like blood. Of course, like the blood that has poured on the street and dried from a vein. The blood that has no use but is frightening to others. My life is now lifeless and agitating like the blood that has poured on the street. So far, I know what notion you have of me but read this letter to the last word to see what I'm suffering.

-I don't have a bad notion. How about you, Negar? Do you have a bad notion?

Negar gives me an angry look and goes on.

Mastaneh and I were friends during high school. Everyone envied our friendship. We were always together. Our families knew one another and there was nothing against our being together. We were like sisters. We knew everything about each other. Either I was at our place or she was at ours. But I don't know what happened to her just out of the blue. We were spending the last year of the high school. For three months, Mastaneh was becoming more depressed and nervous day by day. She didn't even speak to me like before. She didn't visit our house and didn't invite me to her place. She didn't laugh as she used to. When I asked her any question, she didn't answer. One day, I begged her to tell me about her problem. I begged her in a way that I was crying myself but, all the same, she didn't answer me. As we were close, everyone hoped that I could realize why she is upset and depressed. I asked her to see a psychiatrist but she didn't accept it. She also rejected whatever I suggested.

-I dare say she was in love and now I have to listen to this nonsense to see what is wrong with Miss Mastaneh. But she has written it in an interesting way. Now, go on to see where we get.

Negar was still reading without caring about what I was saying.

One Friday, she called me and said: if you want to know what has happened to me, come to park so that I can tell you. I said: Why in the park? Come home, as always. But she didn't accept it and I had to get dressed and go to the park. I went and I waited. I saw her coming nearer. She seemed more depressed than ever. Her face had bruises. As she came closer, I heard her breaths. I had never heard her puff like that. She collapsed on the bench and leaned back. She was exhausted. The sound of her breaths shook my nerves. I asked her to say what this was all about.

But her mouth was open and her face was becoming pale. Then, her breaths all of a sudden became calm and said: take a cab for me, I am feeling bad. Hurry. I freaked out. So quickly, I was asking her what had happened? But she was too exhausted to give any answers. I had a hard time getting her into the cab and once she was inside she passed out. I was crying. There was nothing that I could do. I took her to the hospital. I took her to the emergency section. There was no noise. A nurse came out of the room and said: why has this lady pressed her stomach in this condition? What's you involvement with her? I said: she is a friend of mine. She said: call her husband to come over and follow the procedure for hospitalizing her. I asked: what is the matter? For God's sake, please tell me why should she be hospitalized? She said: why has she pressed her stomach with bandages when she is pregnant?

I was confused and wanted to know what had happened. My whole body was cool. I was dumbfounded. My mind was preoccupied with so many things. But Mastaneh was not that type. We didn't even flirt with any boys, let alone something like that. When she returned, the nurse asked: Did you call her husband? I said: please, for God's sake, if there is something wrong, tell me. Is she that bad? She said: No, she is better now, but it would be better if she could stay in the hospital. I said: No, I must take her home, if her husband knew that she had gone out, there would be a bad fight. She had a troublesome husband, please, for God's sake, let me take her home if it is possible. When the nurse heard what I said, she went back into the room and came back with a doctor. The doctor asked: Did you know that your friend is pregnant? I said: No, she has been having troubles with her husband and she is now staying at her parents' house. She wants to get divorced and maybe that's why she didn't want anyone to know that she's pregnant. The doctor said: that would be dangerous for her and her baby if she was supposed to do this again. I asked: How long has she been pregnant? He said: Over three months, probably.

I went inside to see her. She was lying in bed and she burst into tears when she saw me. I had a cry too.

I soften my voice and say like women: Phew, how sensitive. I am about to cry too.

I didn't expect her to say nothing about it to me but, well, she had not told me and I knew nothing about it. I helped her to get dressed and we were on our way. I want to take a cab but Mastaneh disagreed and said: I want to take a walk. She said nothing about her being pregnant. She only said: I just wanted you to know this. I said: who knocked you up? She sat by the pedestrian and she was about to vomit. She wasn't saying anything. Then, she stood up and walked away. I followed her but she didn't ignored me till she got on a cab and went away. I was left alone. I didn't know what to do. I gave it a lot of thought but I didn't get it. She had been having nausea for some time. Can you believe it? Mastaneh, the girl who was envied by everyone was now like this. Can it be more ridiculous? I just don't know why she didn't tell me how this had happened. I begged so much but she refused to give any hint. When I went home, she made a call and asked me for some help to get rid of it and I promised to help her. But how could I?

She was getting more depressed each day. Before we know it, she was four months pregnant and we could do nothing anymore. I asked anyone that I could think of. I asked my classmates. I asked Mitra, my cousin, who was a slut and with whom I always had a row. I searched the internet for any information on abortion but I found nothing that could solve Mastaneh's problem. Of course, Mitra was little by little getting suspicious. But I just said that it was a mere curiosity. She talked to me about her friends that had gotten pregnant and had found a way to get rid of it. She talked to me in a way as if having such friends is something to be proud of.

She said that being a virgin among my friends means being retarded. You don't know how much I hated Mitra. Such a dirty person and my uncle never thought about taking care of her while my aunt was only too obsessed with parties and showing off and her dear daughter did whatever she could. She wore bad make-up and wore stupid dresses that caught everyone's eyes. So, I cannot put her dirtiness in words. I myself doubted if she was a virgin. Once I asked if she was tired of being a virgin like her friends. In response, she only smiled. Her dirty mouth always had either the alcohol or cigarette stink. When she died, it was clear that she wasn't a virgin. I hate her so much that I don't remember what I was saying.

-I had lost track of what she saying too.

I told one of my classmates that my cousin had just married and was pregnant but did not want a baby yet and she gave me a phone number to a woman doctor and told me to call her and talk to her but first I had to introduce myself and tell her how I had got the number. So we called her. A woman picked up the phone. We told her about our problem and she asked how old my cousin was and for how long she has been pregnant and how many times she has gotten pregnant and more questions. After all, she said: Look, Miss, tell your cousin that it would cost a lot. If she can pay, I give an address. If she can't, don't take my time. When I asked about the cost, I felt dizzy and got off the phone. I told Mastaneh and she backed away too. We did not have that much money. I saw my classmate again and said: my cousins says that the doctor was asking for too much money and I don't have that much. She said that she knew a woman who uses old methods but it could be dangerous and she takes less money. I asked: what do you mean by old methods? She said that she didn't knew exactly. But methods like inserting feathers into a womb or consuming herbal medicines that raise the blood pressure and lead to miscarriage. But when she talked about the things she had hear or perhaps had seen, my heart was trembling. It was dangerous. We neither had money to visit the doctor, nor the heart to go the woman that my friend had introduced. She said that she must go with us for this one. But I didn't want her to know that this was Mastaneh's problem and not my cousin's. And so, the unlucky day came.

-Aha, I think it will get very funny from here, Negar. Go on so we can have a little laughter.

We were sitting in the class when Mastaneh got sick and asked the teacher to let her go out. I wanted to follow her but the teacher didn't allow me to. She was giving me a bad look. I think she had sniffed something. A quarter after Mastaneh went out, the bell rang. I ran to the school yard but couldn't find Mastaneh. I went to the toilets. One of the girls said in which toilet she had gone and hadn't come out. First I thought she was still feeling nauseous. I stuck my ear to the door. I heard groans. I knocked at the door but she didn't make a noise. I pushed the door and struggled to open it somehow. When I went inside, I was shocked. I was going crazy. Mastaneh was unconscious, leaning backward and her eyes were white while she was bleeding between her legs. The bloody feathers caught my eyes. I blamed myself a lot for letting her know how she could deliver with feathers. I didn't know what to do. Or could I do anything? My eyes were full of tears.

-I have tears in my eyes too. Give me some tissue papers.

-I followed the blood track to the toilet seat and I saw an embryo there that was covered in blood. At that moment, I scream so loudly that I fainted. Damn Mastaneh. Damn Leila. Damn Mitra. Damn this dirty world. One day, I will have my revenge at last. On all the dirt of the world. Wait and see.

-Well, nothing then, from now on, people must be careful to avoid her vengeance.

I always wonder why she didn't tell me with whom she had sex? That happening is follows me like a tattoo and cannot be erased from my memory. As if an event is tattooed on your mind; an event that is always before your eyes and cannot be forgotten. I was still struggling with that happening, when Mitra died too. One day, they had told my uncle that she had fallen from the ten-storeyed building. They said they have been in a night party where everyone had used X-pills and everyone has been feeling so bad that no one could have known what had happened to Mitra. Mitra was lost too. She was my cousin, though I hated her. With all my hatred, still I loved her. Her death made me more edgy.

-Funeral. Play a drum to make the dead soul happy.

Negar looks into my sleepy eyes and says: Interesting so far, isn't it?

-It was interesting. Very interesting. But I'm so tired now that I feel I am dying. Leave the rest of it for later.

-You always say you're dying. When you come home, or when you sit behind the computer or watch a film. And I don't seem to exist.

I smile and say: No honey, you really do exist. Look at the time. It's midnight. I want to sleep.

-Go to hell. You never really listen to me.

-You mean I don't really listen to you? Maybe, that's because I am a man and I don't have the patience to listen to something for hours like women do. When I leave school to come home, I need to have some time to spend on my own, don't I?

-It's OK. But shouldn't you be with me for a while?

-Aren't I with you? Don't I talk to you after I finish my things? Didn't I listen to the letter you were just reading?

-Well, listen to the rest of it.

-That won't be necessary. We still have tomorrow. Read it tomorrow. A simple letter should not take my sleep away. Look how many pages are left. Should I really stay awake till it's finished? Is it a letter or a storybook?

-She calms down and says: Do you think Mastaneh has done it?

When she can't give me any answers, she takes softer tone of voice and changes the subject.

-I can't tell right now. I feel sleepy. And by the way, there are a lot of lunatics and psychos who do that kind of things. Go to sleep.

-You're picking on me again. Get up, go to the wind and shout "You stupid psychos, why do you have abortions? Come on. Don't be shy?

I look at her. I get up all of a sudden and go to open up the window. Negar knows that I am too insane to have any shame for shouting and saying things like that and she runs to me and says: I'm sorry, my bad. Please, for God's sake, don't make a fuss.

-What's so fussy? I want to shout. That's not anyone's business.

-Stop it. Don't be crazy. Go to asleep. I'm sorry.

I go back to lie in my bed and I close my eyes.

-That would be finished, if you could hold your sleep a little longer.

I stare into her eyes and frown and say: when I feel sleepy, that means I must sleep. If you want to read it, then read it, but I'm not listening. Make yourself tired if you want to.

I keep my ears with my index fingers and look away. She goes to the kitchen. She says things that I cannot hear.

Though I'm dead tired, I wait until she comes to sleep beside me. She knows that she must sleep next to me in bed so that I can put a hand over her neck and the other one over her breasts to fall asleep.

-Where are you then? Come and sleep.

-I don't feel like it. I have works to do. You sleep now.

-Am I to sleep alone? So, you're being obstinate. Ok, then, just remember that I'll make it up to you.

Nastaran says: Do you see now that she doesn't care about you? She even doesn't sleep beside you. See who you're counting on. You call it a faithful wife? A confidante? If you had married me, I wouldn't have treated you like that. I would have touch your hair, and I would have been kind to you, and I would have slept beside you so you could feel that I'm always there for you. I would never bring a letter from my workplace to read for you and make you even more exhausted. No one can understand you like me, Arman. You made a mistake by falling for Negar. Why don't you believe it?

I say: Shut up. She's better than you, no matter what.

-You know well that, for you, I am better than Negar. Forget her. Let her go and come to live with me. Take it easy. You made a mistake and you can make it up now.

-Shut up. Just shut up.

3

-Your wife has cheated on you. If you don't want to believe it, that's you choice but as a friend I wanted to tell you to do something about it and save your face.

-You?

-I told you I'm a friend.

-A friend must have a name too.

-Well, perhaps in time.

-Like when?

-When this mess is over.

It is disconnected. I am a little on edge. Not just a bit, too much. What can be worse in a man's life than his wife cheating on him? I repeat to myself cheating, cheating, cheating. An affair with whom? Where? Why?

My toothache makes me realize that I am gritting my teeth too hard. I open my mouth to take a breath. An delusional image forms in my mind. Like the one image that Tom Cruise had of Nicole Kidman in "Eyes Wide Shut" showing a sailor making love to his wife. I want to try to remember something that revives a sign of cheating but it is hard to remember anything like that when you're being suffocated by the stink of a passenger who's sitting next to you on a bus.

I like to bang my head against the bus window, or against the nose of the old man sitting beside another old man and is telling him loudly about the good old days. They are now about to review the time they were young when they used to have such a fun on Lalezar Street and what they have done and what they want to do. If they were allowed, they very much liked to rob paraffin on their bald heads and wear loose pants and comfortable shoes to go to a cabaret.

One of the old men says: I never went home at night until I had downed a whole bottle of beer and wine. We were happy then, mister. Anyone could do anything they wanted. Everyone minded his or her own business. There was a mosque and there was a bar next to it. The men of god went to a mosque, and the others went to a bar. I worked to earn ten tomans and I had two tomans for fun and gambling. Two tomans were enough for the wife and family and the rest of it was saved for later. But what now? You have to work like a dog and there is nothing in the end. The closed the bars and the mosques are empty too. As the poet says:

I went to a gambling house and I saw all the honest men

To the monastery I went to see all pretending

When I hear such meaningful verses from the lips of old men like them who I guess are as stupid as a mule and think nothing of drinking beers and wine, I like to bang my head against a wall. It could also be that I am a mule to care about these things. I amuse myself with my cell phone. When I call the prank number, I am rejected. Why am I really calling it a prank call? She said she was my friend. But that's what she says. I am not supposed to believe anyone who says they are a friend. So far it has been just a prank call. I try to remember the morning again. I try to imagine every little moment of it because having an affair cannot be understood by one or two words. I must remember all the behaviors again.

Negar said: First your face and hands. You're killing me. Like babies, I have tell you every morning that....

Because she didn't come to sleep beside me, I tried to make it up to her and didn't wash my hands and my face. Yes, that's it. Why didn't she sleep beside me last night? Why did she begin an argument and stayed away from me? I think the first sign of cheating is staying away from a husband or wife. I seem to be getting some clues. The breakfast was ready. To make her early morning bitter, I took a look at the table that was filled with honey, cream, cheese, butter and orange juice and walnut and other things. I said: Is your salary doubled? The things you have put on the table a whole week's breakfast.

From my behavior and my way of talking she realized that I was still upset about the last night. But she didn't react. She smiled and with her own style she said in a childish tone of voice that: No, I made breakfast for my beloved husband so he can eat well and work well.

And I completed her utterance by saying that: So, I make money and give it to you to spend it all in one place, right?

She stopped eating and said: You're mad again? I guess you got up the wrong side of the bed and want to pick on me again. What do you want to say?

I didn't answer her.

Look, you work and I work too. Why do mean by saying that you bring home money and I eat it?

-I didn't make you go to work. Now, how much is that good-for-nothing magazine pays you to make a fuss about it?

She remained silent for a few moments and then looked at me and said: It was a mistake I didn't come to sleep beside you. I was kind of mad. You keep making me angry. I had the right to be mad at you.

One of the reasons why I love Negar is that whenever she makes a mistake she makes confession. I think if there was a confessor in every house, many problems would have disappear. A simple "I'm sorry" and "I made a mistake" can stop many useless arguments. The courage to say "I am sorry" seems to me to be greater than the courage to fight on the front. When she apologized, I stopped annoying her. Now, to hell with all those things, if she has cheated on me and she comes to make a confession to me, should I forgive her?

Then she asked what my opinion was on the letter she had read for me. That girl's letter with those events. I had no idea in particular. It was a letter that a girl had sent to her workplace. They publish one of those magazines in which people write openly about their lives so that someone like a counselor or psychiatrist can find a way of solving their problems. She wanted to speak about the rest of the letter with me and I disagreed and said that I wanted to hear her reading it that night. Though I made fun of it, I think it was an interesting letter. That was how it went on. She brought home the letters that she found interesting and read them for me. Then, when she saw that I was tired of these repeated stories, she spoke about them. I always made fun of her when she brought home so many sentimental letters to read with a lot of passion. Perhaps, that's why she is through with me and is cheating on me. I teased her several times for these letters. But, well, I was right. Most of the letters were from the girls who had fallen in love with a boy for the first time and had been turned down after a while and they thought it was the end of the world. So they wrote their life story saying that boys are mean. They were most of them teenage girls. Well, such things seem very funny to me. Their foolishness made me laugh as they were so quick to fall in love. Was it possible that she was fed up with my teasing her and had cheated on me? But no. I have sometimes said nice things about her letters. I said it was an interesting one when we were talking about her letter last night. I told her that it was differed from the other letters and I wanted to read it to the end. But no. I made fun of her while reading it.

I grin and tell myself: Fool! Can it be that Negar has cheated on you for making fun of her? It is no big deal why she has done so. Now that you have got a clue, just the fact that she didn't come to sleep next to you last night is no little thing.

I scan the prank calls made by the woman in my mind. She called three times. When she first talked about it, I said she had the wrong number and I hanged up. She called later and I picked up and she asked: Aren't you Arman Pakravan?

I said: Yes, I am. But I don't think what you said concerns me and my wife. I hanged up and the third time she called again and now she doesn't answer when I dial her number.

I kissed Negar on my way out and she asked when I would go back.

I was surprised and said: As usual. Why?

She said: Nothing. I'm just asking.

This is another clue. That was how she acted the other night and this is her suspicious question. She knew when I come back home so why was she asking me then? Maybe she needed time to complete her affair. Time is needed to hide everything. Well, this can be another clue. But no, Negar has asked such questions before. Did her affair begin long before that and I didn't know? No, it can't be true that I haven't understood a thing. Now, what should I do about it? As I am thinking about it, the bus arrives at the school bus stop.

I enter the schoolyard. I see the students who are going to their classes. The janitor is sweeping the yard. He smiles and say "hi" when he sets eyes on me.

He shakes his head and says: What are these kids learning at school, Mr. Pakravan? Why aren't they learning not to spit on the yard and drop their litter in the garbage can and....

I shrug my shoulders and say: Teaching those things is not our business. That's their families' business while we sometimes bring it up.

He cleans the sweat on his forehead with the handkerchief that he takes out of his pocket. He takes a sigh and says: it is not just the school. No matter where you go, you see the same thing. The streets are filled with dirt and garbage. I am not educated but I know these things better than them. Half of my life was wasted in a village in animal's shit. I used to clean the stables and I did my homework right there. Can you believe it? But living in a stable didn't make a cow of me. I don't know where they live, they don't even have a cow's intelligence. Are they going to be the future doctors and engineers? Are they going to run this country? The country that....

-OK, don't talk politics, old man. Keep working.

That's how it is everywhere. Everyone who is not satisfied with something goes on to talk about politics and how the country is run. I have heard or read this sentence that the weakness of governments can be seen in places where people talk about politics and not life. And in our beloved country everyone from small kids to old women talk politics.

I enter the room for teachers. I take my note book out of the closet. As I am heading for the class I see Seyed and he says: Hi. Did you see the news last night?

-Hi. No I didn't.

-I wish you'd seen it! There was a report on a Satanist group. I don't know what the atheists were saying. Not only they didn't have any religion, they also said we are the children of the devil. Isn't that ridiculous?

When I was arguing with him about these sort of things, he objected to what I told the kids in the classroom saying that: what you're saying has nothing to do with lessons. Not to mention, it ruins the kids' rights too.

I call the roll. Moradi does not answer. Saberi who is to look after the other kids says that he is absent.

-why?

-Sir, his mother has dropped a baby last night, I mean, she has a baby. He hasn't come today.

The kids laugh. In my class, everyone is so comfy, but I don't let anyone step out of the line.

-Learn to talk properly. This is school, this is not the Mash Ghanbar's Tea-house.

-Sir, you're embarrassing me.

-Then, don't talk like that.

-Well, his mother's given birth. What am I supposed to say? Should I say she has reproduced?

I burst into laughter and say: you can feel free to say his mother has given birth. You don't even have to say things like that in the class. You might as well say that he has problems and he is absent.

I sit for a while and don't do anything, thinking about Negar. what the stranger told me echoes in my mind.

Saberi interrupts: "Sir, aren't you going to teach a new lesson today?"

- "If you don't mind, no, I won't."

- "Then what are we supposed to do, sir?"

- "Do whatever you want. Just don't make too much noise."

I am drowning in my thoughts. I have a headache because I have been giving it so much thought. I try to look at the kids and to relax a little bit, but when I try, I see that Saberi is talking to his friend about the "Unfaithful" but Though they're talking quietly, so I prick my ears and are able to hear some of their story.

"The film was awesome, boy. I'll give it to you tomorrow. What scenes it had!" Saberi acclaims.

Sharafi asks: What was it about?

- "Wait and I'll tell you all about it. In the film, Richard Gere's wife cheats on him. She has an affair with another man..."

He then speaks more quietly and I cannot make out what he is saying any loner, though I try to. I have seen the film and I know all about it. By the way, why was Negar so upset with me for watching the Unfaithful? I had seen many films over and over again but she had never been so upset. She came and nagged a couple of times and asked me repeatedly to turn it off. Maybe watching that film was a burden on her conscience. I don't know why it is so hard to avoid these thoughts.

The kids are now laughing and telling jokes. At some moments I hear them and laugh about their jokes and at other moments I am preoccupied with the thought of Negar and the caller. I dial her number a few more times but she's still not available. The rest bell rings. I go out of the class and I see Seyed.

- "Mr. Pakravan, your classroom is full of loud laughter."

- "Is that a problem?" I challenged.

- "Yes, my students might get the idea that they should be laughing like your students."

- "Laughter is a cure to any disease." I counter.

- "Mr. Literature, think of my class and teaching too. Now, what were you laughing about?"

Although I hadn't said anything, to make him mad, I say

- "I was talking dirty. what about it?"

"For your mother's sake, stop being an intellectual! These kids might get on the wrong track if you keep arguing them each ideas!"

- "I will keep telling them until they find themselves." I retort.

-"How strange. I had heard a couple of times before that you've been taking about sex in your class but I hadn't believed it. These topics let the kids' mind go wrong. What does it have to do with literature, pal?"

-You're a religious man and you are not open these topics. You think that talking about these ideas is standing against the god; so, let's just do our job."

- "For what? What do the high school students need sex for?" he challenges.

- "Well, it is the way of thinking that makes the East and West have a good laugh about you."

- "No, my pal. You don't have a problem with me. It's my beard." He insisted.

- "I like your beard very much. The trouble is your roots. A student in the third year of high school has passed the puberty, hasn't he? He must have some idea of how to deal with puberty, no?"

He stares into my eyes as I do his.

- "You're not doing OK today; you're just having a bad day. By the way, watch your tongue. I'm not the type that allows anybody to insult my personality so casually." I declare.

- "You'd better watch yourself," he replies threateningly.

It's my fault because I like having verbal fights with a bunch of less than intelligent buffoons. Nevertheless, I tell myself: Idiot, do you have nothing else to do other than ask for trouble? This type of people has issues and you make it worse. Damn me." I wonder who might have told him about the talk that we had about sex in our class. Then I say: "well, the same way that I hear about what's happening in Seyed's class, he gets news about my class.

I have been in school from morning till dusk and now I am going home. I am on the bus. And am still frustrated about the prank calls, I didn't teach in any classes. Now while I'm having a mental struggle on the bus, the story of the letter that Negar had read to me comes into my mind again. Maybe to forget the affair. I surrender my mind to something else. Amusing myself recalling the letter she read. The most important part of the letter was the part about a murder, and I very much wanted to know who he'd murdered and where she was at that moment. Had she written it from a cell? But the thought of Negar cheating on me won't leave me alone. I ask myself,'What do you want to do? You'll go home. You look everywhere, thinking Perhaps it has happened in my own house and these will be something left of the affair in the house. The guilty person always leaves a trace behind, no matter what. It can be anything. A branch of flower hidden in a book or a love card or...anything. Then I will sit with her when she comes home, kiss her as always but perhaps with a little hatred. Then suddenly, I will speak up and ask whether she has cheated. Negar, will become pale and lose herself stammer and want to deny everything. She will have to give up when she sees that I am serious, and will see that she has to run. As she's about to go out through the door, I will stop her and hold up the knife I have prepared and will see nothing but blood. Then maybe she'd be so scared and she'd jump out of the window. I hope this will happen. Then I won't have to blame myself. But what if they don't believe that she did it herself and accuse she? No, idiot, that can't be done. Go home and watch a horror film or the Unfaithful so she'd have to nag about it again. Then when Negar returns, keep watching the screen and don't look her way. As usual, don't go to her and let a fight begin. Then, she'll come and complain that I have forgotten to kiss her or she will complain that I'm watching the same film over and over again. I won't answer her. Whatever she says, I will not care, until she gets mad. then you will get up and ask her "What do you care if I kiss you or not?" she will then ask what I mean. I will tell her and attack her, strangle her, without any noises; then I will cut her body in pieces and put her in a suit case, like the leading character in Hedayat's novelette "The blind owl" who cuts the ethereal woman into pieces and crams her into a suit case. This will be better. Yes, better. Why should you go to jail? Then I will lose her somewhere, maybe you feed her to the stray dogs. A woman who cheats on her husband must be fed to the stray dogs and.... or I will just go home without saying a word, put her stuff in a suit case and put it out in front of the door. When she comes home, I will just tell her that I know everything. "Get lost and don't come back here." No, don't do this either. First try to find the shitty guy who's been having an affair with her, and then, maybe like Richard Gere in the film, I will could trap him somewhere and blow his brains out.

This makes me recall what Shahi was saying in his weblog: "Why shouldn't there be a hedge around the concepts of our existence? Why should we let anyone rob our good intellectual concepts and put something else in their place?"

I ponder further: Negar, me, cheating, the intruder, the intruder, now an idiot like me, I have been wasting my whole time on a prank call from someone that I don't know and I have no idea why I must lose my whole confidence and think foolishly. How stupid of me, I make fun of others for their thoughts and I'm now having the same ridiculous thoughts. With my fist I want to punch myself in the nose! "Why should lose my confidence so easily? Why should I forget all my love and faith in Negar only for a prank call?"

I hate myself for these ideas. I am sick of myself. I say a few times: "I am a fool. If I weren't one, then I wouldn't have such ideas." But I must know where the problem is coming from.

I insert the key into the keyhole, and I am a bit nervous. I want to pull myself together, not do anything stupid, or say something stupid. Then I hear the robotic voice of Mr. Shahi; it goes into my ears and scrapes my brain.

"-Hello. Mr. Teacher. I hope you're not tired."

I saw Mr. Shahi in the morning on the stairs as I was walking out. He had fresh bread. The moment he saw me he stuck the thingy to her throat and said: "Oh, Wow Mr. Teacher. How are you? Good morning to you. Have some fresh bread."

"-No thanks. I've had breakfast already."

"-Come and see me in the afternoon. I have an important job."

His important job is nothing other than to present the same philosophical theories or political arguments that makes me sick at times and at other times causes me to think wisely.

I say: "I took your time yesterday. Let's do it some other time."

"-I ought to show you something very important, I think. I'm losing it. Let me show you. Listen to me and maybe then I could cry out and have a rest!"

Perhaps, because I want to be calmer when I go home, I pull the key out and enter Shahi's house. It is clean as always. I don't know anything about his past because he never says anything about his life. I only know that his wife was killed in an accident and that he's real hush about it, and that his son was also killed in the war. Sometimes, when he talks about his wife, he also says "God-bless the martyr." I once asked what he meant by the word 'martyr', but he just continued talking without answering. But I really wanted to know was why he used the word 'martyr' to refer to his wife.

As usual, he takes me straight to his computer, never inviting me into his other rooms. He has set up two chairs next to one another. There are some fruits on the table besides the chair and the computer is right in front of us. He has a speedy internet.

He then opens up his *weblog* and says "See what I've written. I'll be back when you finish reading it."

He goes to the kitchen.

It's very interesting when I visit your weblogs and see that many of you think lightly of God. You even ridicule him. Some of you talk about the god himself and support the nature of god only to say that god only knows you and the others must drop dead. I hear words from you that make god ashamed even more than the words from the atheists. Some of you have even opened a business under the name of god and deceive the naïve people. What's on your mind? What on earth has given you such a pride and you don't see anybody above you. Look at you. A body made of bone and flesh and blood. That' all there is to it, and a brain that has been bestowed upon you as a gift to think. If you have power, money or any privileges and you don't know yet that all those things are nothing and you're so proud to think that you have everything in control, then you're the real loser. Everyone's gone and you'll be gone too. Then, what answer can you give god?

You think that death is a few steps further than it is to the others. No, you don't think like that. You think that death is an imaginary tale for you and a real story for the others. Imagine death as someone who is holding a gun to your head and pulls the trigger whenever he so chooses. Maybe you let go of you claims when you have such an image in your head.

Death is always with you. If you keep this in your mind, then many of your indecent jobs and your claims wouldn't take shape. The home in this world is for sale even if you're staying in it. What's so attractive in this world?

I go on reading the text, but without any of the patience and energy like the previous texts. However there are sometimes some pretty good sentences. Mr. Shahi comes back with a tray and two cups of tea. Some of the tea is pouring out because his hands are trembling. "Did you read it?"

Without waiting for my answer, he asks: "how is it?"

"-It's interesting." These days there are lots of people who claim to be in touch with god, but as you once said, they're too shy to say that they are a god, otherwise they would have said a thing like that."

He elaborates: "They strip the foolish people of all their possessions. Today, I read on one of these sites where a guy has called himself a savior and has close to thousands of disciples. He has also abused some girls and women. I really don't know what our educated people have done with their intelligence not to think about the simplest and clearest problems and are so naïve to....forget it. Damn them all! I asked you to come over today because I wanted to show you something."

After being his friend for a year, I still don't know what thoughts he has. Sometimes he passionately praises the monarchy and says "What an era it was", and then, out of the blue he starts to blurt out many curse words about it , then he praises the revolution, and then throws out more curse words for all of them. There are pictures of Naser Al-din Shah on his cups of tea and on the wall there is a photo of his son in pilot's uniform standing upright in front of a fighter jet. He says the photo was taken before the very mission in which his son was martyred. He himself is clean and punctual like military people. His face is always close-shaven and his clothes ironed. He opens another site. He pens a webpage. The empty spaces of some photos are now on the page.

"-What's with the photos?" I ask.

He looks at me. His eyes wet with a wave of tears that refuse to fall. I read the footage below each photo. I cannot breathe. I don't know if I should believe it or not. I want to puke. I manage to control myself. I look at Shahi.

"-Should I believe this?" I ask.

He nods: "It's the plain truth."

He doesn't look at the screen. Maybe he's seen them so many times that he cannot take it anymore. Instead he stares at me, perhaps, wanting to read my thoughts in my face.

I cannot look any longer at those intolerable photos and look instead at Mr. Shahi. The photos are from a restaurant in a Southeast Asian country showing people having human embryo and there are also photos are from a kitchen where the chefs are busy cooking the embryos with unspeakable passion. I have no idea why the man or woman who is chewing the embryonic flesh has a smile on their faces. The say men aren't cannibals unless they are forced to. Poor Hitler has been painted black, but in my opinion, Hitler's dog is worth more than such conscienceless people. For all we know we could find one who writes anti-war articles or boast about human rights among these man-eaters.

In the explanation about the photos, it explains the embryos were sold to the restaurants for thousands of dollars and the restaurants in turn charge even more when they sell them to the customers. My hands are trembling, My eye-lids vibrating. My body is wet with sweat. I want to shout, or perhaps cry.

He touches my shoulder and says: "Isn't it an insult to us that these cannibals are also counted as humans? You might also think how anima are some of them. But don't make any mistakes, if you call them animal then you are insulting animals. Wait and let me show you." He opens a file with your photos in it. He shows the first photo.

"-These photos have been taken by a photographer named "Gerry van der Walt" from Africa. Look. This is wild life. A female lion has hunted an animal. This is how her nature is. She kills to fill her stomach. Now, the next photo.

The lion that is ripping apart the belly of the prey gets it that the animal has been pregnant. She takes the baby out of her belly. View the following photos.

She doesn't eat the baby. She puts it away. But view the last photo. This lion falls and dies without having a slice of the prey.

The experts say they cannot find any reasons for
the lion's death, apart from saying that the lion was
so ashamed of what she'd done that she chose to
die. When an animal hunts by natural instinct and
sees that the prey is pregnant, it dies. But, what
should we say about these dirty bastards? I think
we would be insulting animals if we called them
'animals'. You tell me, what should we call them?"

He looks directly at me. He is expecting to hear
something from me. But I can't say a word. What
can I say? Whatever he says this time, I'd agree with
him.

He shakes his head and says: I am sorry that I have
showed you these things. I ask myself what this
world wants from us? What do we want from it?
You know what I think after seeing these photos? I

think God's dead. He would have done something, if he wasn't dead. If I wish this world would sink like the time of Noah, don't laugh at me. Since I have seen these pictures I tell myself that God has no sense. Either he has lost his powers, or his mind. Why should my heart be filled with sorrow and the faces of these dirty bastards show smiles? These words of mine go against what I read for you yesterday. But how would god expect us to worship him despite seeing these pictures? How am I to keep the faith in god alive in my heart? How can I be ever in love? God is my witness, anywhere I went to give a lecture, whether it was in the country or abroad, I shouted that it was not hard to be human. But god took my throat. I don't know why. Perhaps I have said something inappropriate and god has left me like this. Now to say a couple of words, I have to stick this electrical thing to my throat to make my words. Now everyone is wearing something and calling themselves 'human'. One wears the uniform of religion and one wears the uniform of battle. But I have not seen humanity in any of them. The bastards have built a United Nations and keep putting out noble mottoes, but, damn them all! They cannot protect the animals' rights, let alone human rights. If they could, things like that wouldn't happen so clearly.

His chin is shaking. Tears are pouring from his eyes. He barely seems to breathe, or perhaps I cannot hear his breaths. One can't let the heat of grief in and out of a small hole in the throat. Still I am not saying anything.

He goes on: "I guess this world is falling apart because the ones who must teach the ways of humanity, love and monotheism to the people are silent or have been silenced. Then, the others who see their empty place, become more Catholic than the Pope and appear everywhere and claim anything, even being god. They're the ones that make this life worthless. A mind empty of god, of love, a life which is but worthless and hollow."

I wanted to leave, but I am now sitting and don't intend to leave. He goes to the kitchen and fetches me a glass of water and says: "Lucky you! You have wife on your side and when you see her you forget the sorrows of the world and you're in another world. But what about me? I have lost everything that I had. Wife, son! For many years I sat behind this computer and looked everywhere in the world. I saw all the misdemeanors. I died and lived again. One of these days, my guess is my heart will stop for all these dirty creatures. Perhaps, this is the end of the world, where we are now. Go and attend to your wife. Go now, before she worries about you."

I look at the glass without a top. The top was flowing over when he brought it because his hands trembling. I tells myself: it is age that makes his hands tremble. Or was it seeing such scenes? I wanted to ask where he had given his lectures all these years. I wanted to know what he'd done to make a living. But I knew that my questions would get no answers unless he brings them to himself.

I don't feel like leaving him yet I'm also not in the mood to stay. I feel a frozen creature. I finally stand up with a little trouble and I go home. There is not enough time to think about my going in and seeing Negar. Especially because I have got a more important thought now. No matter how painful an affair might be, it cannot be more painful than the fact that some people are enjoying eating human embryo somewhere in the world.

For a moment, I think "I'm killing myself worrying too much about the world. Forget it, go right now and take Shahi's hands and put your hands round his back and begin to dance Tango. Get up, fool. What's good about being crazy anyway? It is good at times like this that get rid of all the pains in the world. Go and ask him to perform the Baba Karam dance for you. I'm sure he knows how to do it. But, no, my insanity is not of this type."

I open the door. Negar is standing in front of me. With a frowned face like a dog that is about to bite. She says: "Why are you so late?"

"-I was with Shahi."

"-But you were there yesterday. Why did you go there today? Tell me. Tell me more lies!"

I stare into her eyes. They are a little red. Her chin is shaking. She suddenly bursts into tears. "Arman, why are you cheating on me?"

Nastaran says "Then, she found out that you were cheating on her after all?"

" Shut up. I haven't had an affair with anyone."

"-How interesting. Then, being with me is not an affair? Then, what shall we call it?"

"-Ah, that's enough. There you go again?" I snap impatiently.

She laughs and twists her hair around her left finger, covers her nose and collapses in the chair. She looks sharp, touches her thigh, and asks: "How much do you love me?"

I smile and reply: "How much I love you? That's a ridiculous question! I hate you. You get it? I hate you."

"-You're just bringing more excuses. Tell me you don't want me and let me go." She pouts.

"-I think I've said it before."

"-No, you have not."

"-Well, I'm saying it now." I state.

"-No. You're mad now. I'm sure you love me. As usual. As before Negar came along, right?"

"-No, I only love Negar now. Just Negar."

"-I'm the only one who loves you with all her heart, not Negar. You're my whole existence. You know that well enough. You gave me life. I fell in love with you and you did too. You said that yourself. But I don't know what's coming to you now."

"-I asked you to stay with me but you said no. everything was finished then. You get it?" I reminded her.

"-Well, it was my mistake. Now, I'm here to stay with you forever. Till the world ends. You just have to ask me one more time. Just one more time. "

"-But it's just too late. Negar has filled your place in my heart. Don't bother."

"-You know well that I am your real lover." She insists.

"-Negar is also in love with me. With her whole heart. I'm in love with her too." I assert half-heartedly.

I stop talking so she will stop babbling. But she doesn't. She gets up and goes to the window and begins to tell her story about her boss who keeps bothering her. She cleans the curtains while saying they are supposed to go out and have a date in a restaurant in Darakeh and talk about things I don't want to hear. She says maybe she will go to his place and…

I look at her angrily: "Do whatever you want. The hell with that! This way, you will help me forget all about you."

But can anyone forget her first love? Can one forget the shakes of the first time one falls in love? This is one of those events that, like the girl with letter has put it, will remain on one's mind like tattoo. Forever.

She gets up, grabs her bag, plunges her hand in her pocket, and says: "I'm leaving."

-Better.

Then she turns, smiles and says: "I want to say I'm leaving and won't be back, but because I already miss you I can't say so."

"-I wish you could say it and would go away forever."

"-Even if I say so, you would be the one who'd come for me. I know you're mad at me. Don't be scared. Everything about me and my boss was a lie. I wanted to see how you would react." She confesses coyly.

"-Everything with you is a lie."

"-Whatever you do, just don't humiliate me or...."

"-Or what?"

"-Nothing."

"-No, spit it out." I demand; "or what? What are you going to do?"

"-You know bitches like me can do a lot."

"-Now you're saying that you are a bitch. What the hell are you going to do?" I demand.

"-I'd jump in your life and make everything like hell."

"-Look, you know better, you can't do a damn thing. So, what are you babbling about? Why are asking me to humiliate you even more?"

"-You think I can't do a damn thing? Then, let's see what I'm capable of." Now defiant.

"-You can't do a damn thing." I taunt, but by now my whole thoughts are mixed up. "Why is that I can't let her out of my damn mind and forget her? I don't lack anything in my life, so what's pushing me towards that slut?"

4

I was still lucky that Mastaneh could pull it off, otherwise I really didn't know what to do if she had died on me because after that event, my life turned black. Just too black. Everybody assumed I knew everything, and assumed me to be guilty. It was all blame. My dad was also hitting me for the same thing; my friendship with Mastaneh was finished. To escape the whole adventure, to escape Mastaneh's family, who thought it was my fault, we had to move into a new house in another neighborhood. But I had left my soul with Mastaneh forever.

"-Oh, poor thing. She's had such a hard time." I say. " It gives me heartache."

Negar says: "Please, stop being funny."

"-I try but I won't promise."

I couldn't see Mastaneh anymore or speak to her. Her cell phone was always turned off, and once, when I was too scared to call them on their family phone, a man picked up saying that they had left the house. All my hope for finding her was gone. None of my classmates knew her where-about either. My parents didn't trust me any longer. So, everything about me was controlled. I wasn't free like before. It was as I was pregnant, like I had had an abortion. Sometimes I wondered what they would do to Mastaneh, if this was how they treated me. In my new school, I didn't make an friends. The trouble with Mastaneh and Mitra had pressured me so much that I could no longer think of having a social life, so I was depressed and lonely, that is until I came to know Leila after some time, a classmate who was reserved and lonely like me. I don't know, maybe this similarity attracted us. We became friends. After all, I told her what had happened to me and Mastaneh and she shared details about her life: she was living with her older sister; their parents were dead and they had decided to live together and hadn't allowed anyone to make rules for them, and Sheila, her older sister, had become a prostitute to make a living.. Not surprisingly, her sister has AIDS, and she knows, but she does not tell anybody and keep doing this "work".

"-I believe it. How about you, Negar? Do you believe this nonsense too? No?"

I tried to persuade Leila to keep Sheila from doing it again. She said she had tried to, but when she had opened her wrists before her eyes, she had backed away. Leila said she wanted to introduce her to a medical center and when she had known about it, she decided to forget about it. We were like each other. Confused and helpless. Sadness and helplessness was what Leila and I had in common. We tried to be confidante to one another, but our friendship didn't last long enough and Hassan Jighil entered our life; a bad thug who annoyed us on our way to school and said things that I am too ashamed to express here. But the thug didn't stop at that. He annoyed us every day and wasn't scared of anybody. We had even heard that he had beaten the policemen who wanted to arrest him and had run away after that. He was put away a couple of times only to be released after some time.

"-Damn! Oh, sorry, I was supposed to shut up and listen."

Our story had just begun. Hassan Jighil didn't give up. He wanted me and Leila to spend a night with him. We freaked out whenever he showed up. It was no use swearing at him, no matter how many times, because Hassan Jighil wasn't afraid of anybody and the people who saw us didn't dare to step in or just giving us an insinuating look as if it was we who were asking for trouble. We had a fight with that bastard every day! We tried to change our route so not to set eyes on him again. Sometimes we made it, and sometimes we didn't. He conjured our way every time and there were more dirty words and pranks. But we had to do something, so we made a plan. Maybe it was the craziest, maybe the bravest plan of my life.

"-Were they experts on making plans?"

Negar looks at me for a couple of moments so I keep quiet. She goes on.

I suggested that we pretend to give him what he wants: We take him home. Leila didn't accept it, but I urged her to play along. Leila wanted to know what we would do next? I said we'd figure out something to keep him away from us forever, so we bravely worked out our plan. We took Hassan to Leila's place. He said he wanted to bring his friend, but we refused. We said either you come alone or you can forget it. So he came alone. He was very drunk and declared: "What good girls! They themselves invited me to their place. I hadn't ask too much of you. I just wanted us to play husband and wife a little."

Leila was gasping: "Do what you want to do quick and then beat it."

He looked at Leila, then me. I think he preferred Leila to me with her blue eyes and soft shiny skin and her slim body while I was too skinny and had a freckled face.

"-What an appetite!"

He took Leila's hand. Leila was trembling like leaves. She was scared and so was I, but we were well prepared and had gone through our plan together. Leila and Hassan Jighil went to the bedroom, he threw her on the bed and jumped on her like a hungry wolf. I was shaking all over my body; It was getting out of hand! Hassan Jighil was naked and the scorpion tattoo on his back scared me away. I thought if I got close to him, the scorpion would sting me. That's stupid, isn't it? But, well, I was frightened. I was seeing Leila's anxious face. Hassan Jighil didn't even noticed me then. He had torn her dress apart but according to our plan she was hanging on, waiting for my move. I rushed to my bag, took the bottle out, opened it and went back to the bedroom. By the time Hassan was on Leila and he had his back to me. I didn't wait; poured the acid on his back. For a moment, he froze up, then screamed his nuts off. Leila and I kept our ears so he was screaming: "It's burning! it's burning!" We didn't know then what we were supposed to do about his loud screams. He was jumping up and down until he saw me, then like a wild bull, he assaulted me trying to strangle me to death. I was breathless. We were fighting when I heard something breaking and his hands around my neck were loose and he fell on the floor. Leila was standing with the remainder part of the glass vase in her hands. Blood was pouring from his head but was still conscious. He had shut up though and was tossing and turning like a wounded rattlesnake. There was blood all over him. He staggered towards me on his hands and legs. I was scared, so I grabbed the metal bucket near the bed and hit him on the head, which gave me immense pleasure. I hit him again and again until his head was like a squeezed pomegranate. Leila, not moving a muscle, stood like a branch until she suddenly vomited and ran out of the room. I went out too and locked the door. My heart was threatening to jump out of my chest, but what else could we do? Like mad people we paced here and there. After about an hour, we couldn't hear anything from inside the room, so Leila said we should do something. "What if he dies?" I asked: "Do you really think he could still be alive after hitting him like that? Even if he is alive, the acid would have given him a long and painful death." We had to do something, but what? The floor was covered with blood and we couldn't hide his dead body anywhere. We waited till Sheila arrived.

I say: " I need a glass of water."

"-Wait. I'm still reading."

"-I want some water. By the way, that's enough for tonight."

"-Why? Wait a little and let me finish this. There's not much left."

"-I don't know. I think this letter was mostly just a bunch of lies."

"-Lies? What makes you say that?"

"-I just can't imagine two brave girls like them taking their revenge on this guy. Do you believe it? Isn't her account of what was happening with Mastaneh too imaginary? The toilets in many schools and universities are filled and are not designed to let anyone drop a human embryo in them. That Mastaneh didn't tell her how she got pregnant, of course a lie. She knows about it but she is afraid to write about it even in a letter. Then again the life of Leila and Sheila is also unbelievable. How is that, orphaned and alone sisters, one goes to school and the other becomes a hooker? Isn't that imaginary? But the fact that many have AIDS and still work as a prostitutes is not surprising. Many of them form an obsession and go on doing that once they know that they have the disease. Even they might have sex with others without charging them. They do it to have their revenge on this kind of life and transmit the disease to others. This is a fictional story. A story in which the writer has blended the truth with fiction. It's just that." I asserted with finality.

"-You're trying to get a rise out of me again? Let me read the rest of it. And you just listen. I didn't ask you to find faults with the letter like a critic. Just wait. Hear what they do with the dead body."

"-Please, don't read it now." I plead.

"-Funny guy."

"-You're the one being funny. Fetch me some water." I demanided.

She goes to brings me some water, but stays in the kitchen so long that my thirst begins to kill me. Long enough for me to recall the moment when Negar said: "Arman, Why have you been cheating on me?" In a flash, I was about to lose control. But I hadn't been having an affair, so why would I be losing it. I said nothing.

"-I didn't know you to be so mean to cheat on me someday." She declared and went to pack her things.

"-Are you Okay? Do you know what you're saying? What's the story of cheating? What the hell is wrong with you?" I demanded.

"-I am going to my mother's house." Was all she would reveal.

"-You can go. That's all right with me. But first tell me what's going on."

"-Why are you pretending? I know the whole thing. I know everything. Still, you're not going to admit it? Well, if you don't want me, just say so." She whispered.

I turned up my voice as much as I could: "Who's said that I don't want you? Who's been telling you that?"

I was loud enough to make her feel that the neighbors might smell a rat, so she tried to calm me down. She said: "Hissss! The neighbors are going to hear that!"

"-The hell with that! Tell me what's happening, then go to your mother's house."

It was then she showed me her cell phone: "Someone has been calling since this morning and she's been giving me clues. She has talked about the whole thing told me where you two have been. Even told how much she knows about you. She talked about your favorite foods and all your habits and your favorite poets and writers. She even said that you have a scar on your shoulder. I think no one can see the scar on my husband's shoulder on the street! She then asked me to leave your life because there is no place for me in it."

I took the cell phone from her hand and checked the number. It was the same number that had contacted me.

I showed her my cell phone and the number. My hands were shaking with anger. "I have not cheated on you, but what about you? Have you been cheating on me?" I demanded.

Negar became pale when she saw my anger. "What does that mean? Me? Me?"

I was shouting now: "Idiot! You fool! You stupid fool! This means someone is trying to ruin our relationship. What a stupid girl I have married. Why should you lose your confidence in me with a couple of words? Why? Yes, she called me too. She said you're having an affair. I doubted too. But after giving it a lot of thought, I asked myself why I would trust to an unknown caller? But what about you? You were fooled to forget everything and lose your whole confidence over a prank call. That's it! This caller is even crazier to call the both of us." I was trembling with anger now.

"-I don't believe you. Who can this person be who knows about the scar on your shoulder?" She challenged.

I was hoping she would be more reasonable after what I said but her question proved otherwise.

Quietly, I tried to calm her. "Don't argue with me. Go to your mother's house. But I don't have any doubts about you, or myself. I'm just sad you do not trust me enough to know that I am not the type. I won't share even a little romantic chat with a woman." I self-righteously asserted.

I went to the bedroom, slammed the door and lay on the bed. I felt like crying, not for what had happened, but for the confidence that I had failed to plant in Negar's heart so our relationship couldn't be broken by such a stupid move from someone. Lives that go by the routine are no good. There has to be some fights and arguments so the partners can know each other better. This made me understand that what I'd done to gain her trust wasn't enough. But where had I failed? I have to think about it. I have to find a way or create one.

When I come home, I had wanted Negar to come to me, to take my bag, and help me take off my jacket. I wanted her to ask how I was doing, hand me a drink, and ask what had being going on at school and, instead of saying nothing has happened, I would tell her about the prank call and what I'd heard and she would laugh and say that she'd been called too. Then, she would kiss me and say that it must have been a fool to call the both of us.

I am not that romantic. I just want Negar to ask me to sit with her to talk, she would tell me what had happened and I would tell her instead of arguing. We would sit down and think about who has been so close to us, so close that she could know about the scar on my shoulder. Or, when she told me that the caller even knew about the old scar on my shoulder, I would lie like someone other than me must knew that there is a freckle on her left boob. Maybe if I'd said that, the argument would not have come so far. But when a woman starts an argument, one can't have his turn unless she wants him to. As I was "wishing", I noticed that I hadn't heard the exit door.

I wondered: "Does it mean that Negar hasn't left yet? Why is that? Maybe while I was "wishing", she went out and I didn't hear." While I was looking at the door a little surprised, Negar opened it and came into the bedroom. Her cheeks were wet with tears. She lied down next to me and put her head on my arm and began to sniff. I didn't say a word, because it was the best time to think for the both of us. I didn't know what was going on in her mind that made her believe it was just a prank call.

Why is it that my simple life creates obsession for others, so much so that they make a move like that? Perhaps, the simplicity of life is the key to their jealousy. Perhaps, it is only their hobby. There are many who enjoy seeing the lives of other people fall apart so they can talk and laugh about it and this is just a hobby for them. I think that's it. But how obsessive must this hobby be if she knows all about my style and even the scar on my shoulder?

"-Water."

-My thoughts lose their order.

-When you fetch a glass of water, it is like going to a water spring.

"-Well, then, go and fetch a glass."

"-Ok, sorry, I'm sorry."

"-That's all right. It had better be the last time though."

I wake up exhausted; Negar is still sleeping. I fill the kettle with water and put it on the heat. I go to the bath. When I come out, the breakfast table is ready. I sit on the chair.

Negar says: "Good morning, darling."

"-Good morning."

"-Where's the 'darling'?"

"-Good morning, DARLING. Now, are you satisfied?"

"-Yes."

She laughs and she wants to scratch my hand with the knife in her hand when I pull my hand back. Of course, if didn't pull it back, she wouldn't really do it. But, anyway, this is the rule of the game, I fear and she moves. A game is something you should know about even if it is funny; otherwise it will turn into a fight.

She sits in front of me and says: "How was school?"

"-As always."

"-That's it? Tell me who's coming, who's going. How about that?"

"-It's just school. Like always. You tell me."

"-OK, then. Elnaz was kind of down yesterday. I asked her why? She said it seems that they can't have a baby. She asked me not to tell anyone."

"-Aha, so you didn't tell anyone about it?" I asked facetiously.

"-No, I didn't. You're not anyone; you're my hubby. Oh, I have some other news. I saw Zahra was on the phone and was talking for about half an hour with someone she didn't want anyone to know about. Then it slipped out of her tongue that she's has a boyfriend."

"-Who is Zahra?" I asked.

"-The one I said has pretty blond hair and..."

I interrupted. "Oh, I see."

She used to talk a lot about her coworkers so I knew all of them although I had never seen any of them but she had explained how they looked like so much that I could perhaps recognize them at once if I saw them. It could be also the case that Negar has told some of them about my scar and this has given them a chance for the prank call. What is heard between them is a secret; no one is supposed to know about them. But the news always comes to me the thoughts that Negar also tells them about our things bothers me.

"-Zahra is in love with him too. She says he is not a bad boy but she doesn't know him well." Negar continues.

"-So, where was this nice guy found?"

"-I guess they have met on the street." She speculates.

"-That's interesting. So she writes a lot of these warning tips in the magazine about not having a boyfriend and all that stuff and this concerns only the people, right?"

"-You're being picky again? Can you stop picking on our magazine for once?"

"-Did I say something wrong? I don't understand whether your magazine is against boy and girl relationship or not."

She presses her lips for a second and that sweet spot on her cheeks shows up. "How should I know? Not all relationships are bad, they could be good too. How on earth can we know?"

"-Bravo! That's what I'm saying, that you try to scare boys and girls out of their relationships. How could you know that they don't come to any good? Why don't you publish two or three about how smart these girls are in testing the boys and jumping to conclusions instead of publishing thousands of good-for-nothing stories about girls being cheated? Like this letter that you're reading, why don't you dare to have it published?" I am testing her.

"-But you're assuming that it is a bunch of lies."

"-I didn't say that it is all a lie. Even if it is a lie, it's still good to publish it to give women a little courage. Why do you keep using stories from miserable women? Isn't there any woman in this country that has positive thoughts in life that you want to show? You have written all about these miserable fates and now everyone thinks having a relationship outside home means misery and trouble. But you never explain a good relationship to them. You keep reporting on fake lovers and their destiny." I'm a bit defensive now.

Negar opens her arms and proclaims: "Wow! Mr. Teacher! How nice of you to say so. Where have you been keeping yourself all this time? What a pity that we hadn't met you till now. I won't let you go out anymore. If people would find out how what a genius my crazy husband is, they might hurt him. No, honey, it's too dangerous to leave the house anymore!" She proclaims flippantly.

I stare directly into her eyes I say: "You're a lot funnier than me."

She smiles. "What are we going to do? You say they are no good. All right then, but we are being strangled by intellectual poems and novels. We really can't get a clue about how to love from them. Housewives have nothing to do with philosophy, complicated novels, and principles. We're talking to them in their own language, they cannot understand you, yet you're expecting us to publish stories that are so hard to understand that they would have to meditate to get to the heart of the matter. Where are you standing, darling? Most women sleep tight at night because they're so exhausted and early in the morning they're still exhausted and have to go to work."

"-I didn't say that everyone must read professional stories. I just believe that they must solve some problems. The defeatism in your stories will not do anyone good. They won't introduce any new experiences to your readers. If you're writing about losing, write in a way that exposes them to losing so they can take advantage of it. What I'm saying is when you have ten stories about losing; you must also have at least a few stories that are about winning."

She now has her hand under her chin: "Who do you think I am when you talk to me like an expert? I am only an ordinary employee. Look at me. I am your wife. That's it. If you're bent on having an expert conversation then feel free to come over to our office and tell it all to the editor. I haven't read any literature and I have no idea what you're saying."

"-Forget it. I must be crazy to argue with you."

"-Bravo, darling. Have your breakfast and don't feel blue. Look on the positive side!" She responds jubilantly.

She's making me angry. That's what she knows best, so at times like this, I look for things to make her mad too.

"-Where are you going?" I ask provocatively.

"-Well, you can tell, right? I am going to my office. What makes you ask?"

"-You mean…"

And I stop saying the rest of it to make her angry.

"-You mean what? Talk."

"-You mean you're not going to your affair now?" I prod.

She picks up the glass of water from the table and sprinkles the water on my face: "You're a real lunatic. You know I hate you to say that and you still say it?"

I succeed in provoking her. It was a bad joke so I get up, and hold her hands. But she pulls them away. I continue to hold her tight and apologize with a kiss. Women are all like that. They overreact very quickly. But they are quick to forgive the man in their life. If god didn't gave women some particular features, life would have ended with Adam and Eve. At least the woman that I have been given has such qualities. We as men might go crazy, and say things that only annoy women, but we have to apology.

"-If you want me to forgive you, you must go out to the park with me this afternoon. " She bargains.

"-Ok, we'll go."

"-I want chips and snacks too."

"-There you go!"

-I would like a saffron ice-cream too.

"-This time, I'm afraid of saying "OK" because you might ask me to buy you that green Manteaux as well." I begin pulling away slightly.

"-How did you find out?"

"-You got nerves, really."

"-Well, you have to buy me the Manteaux. This one has gotten too old."

"-It will cost an arm and a leg. I know it."

"-We haven't even asked how much it costs yet. We can do that. Shall I ask?"

"-No, we will go together."

"- Well done. There is a good boy!" She is victorious.

Her cell phone rings. She grabs the phone and looks at the calling number and then she looks at me.

"-It's that prank call again."

Negar doesn't answer, hangs up. I make her promise me that she won't answer until I come up with an idea. She looks at me in such a way that I cannot tell if I'm being naïve to think that she believes there's nothing between me and the caller.

"I say: Well, then you make the call."

"-But you told me not to." She counters.

"-We're together now. Call her and maybe we will know who's behind this."

She looks away as if she has doubts, then she puts the phone from one hand into another and dials the number.

"-No answer."

She tosses the phone down and says: "This bastard is shaking my mind!"

"-Why are you allowing her to do this to you? Look, you either have confidence in me or you don't. which is it?"

"-I have confidence in you. You get it? But I'd have to know who this is." She's pacing now.

"-For what? I told you not to give a damn about it. She'll let go after a while."

"-Who the hell is she, knowing every detail about you and me?"

"-Look, Negar, listen to me well. I don't know what you're thinking. But I'm not the cheating type and all that stuff. You know better. I didn't think you'd have a change of heart so easily."

"-I told you once, I have faith in you. So, don't talk like that anymore. Don't make me mad. We have to find out who this bastard is."

"-We can trace the call if we ask, but letting it go is our best choice. Being together like we have been in the past will hurt that prank caller more than anything else."

"-Hell if I wouldn't know her."

"-I hope you never get you your hands on her. Damn it. Let it go! Don't blow a fuse for this. The only thing that matters is you and I and we have faith in each other. That's it. You could turn off your cell phone for a couple of days." Problem resolved.

I leave the house. The phone rings. It's the damn caller again. I wonder why she enjoys setting my life on fire?

"-Hi."

"-Hi, prank caller."

"-I wish all the callers were just like me."

"-Like what?"

"-Like being kind enough to others to let them know if their wives were having an affair."

"-Yes, that's right. By the way, do you know that I killed my wife last night?"

There is a pause and then I hear her breathing.

"-You don't take it from me, I guess."

"-When I have killed my wife; this means I have believed you. Now tell me about the man who's been sleeping with my wife. Was it your own husband who has spit you out?"

"-Nope. First of all, I have no husband, and second, if had one, I am so pretty that no one would spit me out! Anyone would be madly in love with me the second they see me." She taunts.

But there's a tremble in her voice which means it is my turn to get a rise out of her this time.

"-Ok, then, what are we going to do now? Do you like us to be together for a night? You have a gentle voice and I wish you have a gentle body too. And it's a lot better that you have no husband. Of course, you must be a widow. I really don't believe that no man has spit you out before because these type of women form an obsession and like to play with the other people's lives. Now, forget all of it. Shall we have a date?"

"-You dirty pig. You take me for a whore? You son of a...."

We are disconnected. Her voice was shaky and I could even sense her sobbing in her last sentence, but I'm not letting her get away with it this time. I dial her number. There is a connection, but she doesn't say anything.

"-Listen well, you poor girl. Negar said you have called her. First of all, I can't guess how stupid you are to call both of us. Maybe you thought it was better to set the both sides on fire, but Negar told me the whole story last night. Everything has been settled between the two of us. I don't know what you're after, but listen to me: If you make one more call, it'll be very easy for me to find you. Then, if I get my hands on you...." I threaten.

I hear a voice from the other side saying: "Hang up! Hang up!"

Again disconnected, but the voice sounded very familiar to me. Gosh, Who was that? I struggle to knowing it. I try to call again but the cell phone has been turned off. It was a familiar voice! Who could it be? Is it that some people have come together to ruin my life? Anyway, I think I frightened them away. I put the cell phone in my pocket and wait for the bus.

The janitor is busy sweeping the school yard.

"-Hello there, Mr. Pakravan."

"-Hi. Hope you're not tired. Hard work."

"-Thank you. There's something I wanted to tell you."

I go closer, "I'm at you service."

"-This is between us but I heard the principal and some other teachers talking behind you back. They were telling the principal that you are saying things that you shouldn't say in your class. The principal said that he will report you if it was proven that you are saying inappropriate things in your class. I felt it was my duty to tell you about this. I have no idea what you have said in the class but, anyway, I wanted you to be careful."

"-Which teachers were saying that?" I asked.

"-Don't ask because I won't say. Just wanted you to know."

"-Thanks. Go on."

I'm head for the teachers' rest room and as I pass I hear some of them talking, my name among their words. However the corridor is too crowded and I cannot eavesdrop. So I go into the rest room where Seyed and three other teachers are sitting in a circle. One of them coughs immediately upon seeing me and Seyed stops talking. I stand in the door for a few moments, give them a chuckle, and turn to leave immediately.

I take the roll and call book, and just as I am going to my class, Seyed says: Hello, Mr. Pakravan, how come you're not paying us any attention?

"- One pays attention to one's pal, not back-stabbing guy."

"-Why are you saying that? Has something happened?" Seyed persists.

"-Nothing has happened. Everything's fine. It's just that I don't feel any good." I answered.

I walk towards my class, am not there yet when I hear some students talking loudly.

"-Everyone just shut up. I'm studying."

"-Four-eyes, you've been studying your whole life, what did you get, huh?"

"-Stop it. Do you think this country is going to be fine because of your chit-chats?"

"-Listen, you wiener nose, you don't know nothing about politics. Then button up your lips. " The tormentors continue.

I wait behind the door for a couple of moments and wait to see that the argument is over but it seems to be getting worse. As I open the door, everyone becomes silent and stands up.

"-Sit down. If your kindness to one another is over, and if this is a class, and not an open market, then with your permission, gentlemen, today's lesson must get started." I command.

No one says a word. When I call the roll, I amuse myself with my stuff from my bag, and the kids start to whisper to each other.

Suddenly Saberi asks: "Sir, it seems you aren't in the mood to teach today either."

I raise my voice: "Teach? For what? Have you learned anything after teaching you so much? Did you get anything?"

A few of them look down.

"-No, I won't teach you. These things that I teach will do you no good. If this is the way you talk, what good is knowing about Hafiz and Molana? We need to just talk."

"-What are we going to talk about, sir?" One askes.

"-About politics. What's your idea? I guess there are many political activists in our class. Now, one of you tell me what was the political talk about?" Ahmadi says: "Nothing, sir. Some of the kids have lost their minds and keep talking about these things. One of them says 'I don't like this guy'. Another says 'I don't like that guy'."

"-Well, what else do they say? Aren't they going to speak themselves?" I query and glance around.

No one speaks.

"-Ok, then, it will be better to speak about 'marriage'."

Still on one speaks. This is enough already. I don't continue knowing that they are sorry.

Ahmadi says, "Excuse us, sir. I swear to God, I don't' want to take your time, but we have heard that Turkey has claimed Molana."

"-This is nothing new. We have had other poets and scientists that have been claimed by other countries."

Saberi says, "But, sir, aren't we going to do something about it, or have we lost the cultural invasion? Then, we must try to prevent cultural invasions. Don't you think this is an invasion on our culture?"

Saberi is one of the kids that is always wiser than his age and sometimes says things that keep my mind busy for hours.

"-I have nothing to say. I can only say that I am sorry about it. I have done my share by sending E-mails to places that are related to this matter. But it has been useless so far. I don't want to say that if you sit and look and think, nothing can be done. I want to say that you should talk too. If you are a weblog writer, then write something about it, if you are a poet, or a writer, or can do anything else, then make a move. Don't just go after jokes and photos and all that stuff on the internet. Don't doubt that if we have patience and try hard in pursuing a goal, we well get the desirable outcome. Don't forget that, as Saber said, they have invaded on our culture. But, make a move. Those who don't, are both traitors and accomplices for the invaders. Cheating is not just a problem in marriage and national subjects. The stupid fool who distorts and puts the historical and religious lessons in the wrong way is also a traitor in the class. That fool is cheating on your beliefs."

"-Hurrah!" Saberi proclaims.

As he bursts into laughter, the kids start laughing too. I cannot control myself, so I laugh too, go to Saber and pinch his ear.

I leave the school, and get a taxi; I want to get home early to have more time to go to the park. I sit next to the cabbie, as the behind door opens and two girls get in. One of them is wearing sunglasses and is talking and says to her companion: "I said 'You dirty pig, that's not the way to talk to a lady'. Then he said: 'I'm talking the talk, honey!' I said, 'look, if you want to step out of the line, I'll have you crushed. He said 'honey, I'm not going to have a fight with you. I suggested we go somewhere alone. Was it a lousy suggestion'?"

I quickly turn around and say: "Look, ma'am, do you think it is right for a respectable lady to speak loudly in this tone of voice in a taxi, right in front of a strange man, engaging in childish talk?"

Both of them stare straight at me, shocked. They didn't expect me to tell them straight. They have worn make-up and look like the dolls that are made up to attract customers. I can even smell their make-up. One girl's nostrils are opening and closing like the nose of a donkey that has not been fed and she says: "You dirty pig! Keep your ears to yourself what I'm saying!"

"-I'm sorry, Miss. You're so loud that even the cigarette seller on the sidewalk is looking at you and is laughing about what you're saying. Just look at him."

She looked at the seller laughing on the sidewalk showing his golden teeth.

Her friend says "Stop arguing with us, Mister. Mind your own business."

Then looks at her friend and says "Let's go in another cab."

"-No! I want to set thing straight with this man."

-I grin and say "Look, I'm not the type that I look to you. If you start to talk like that, right here, I'd...."

I don't go on, saying to myself: "What are you going to do here, turn into the lunatic who's hiding under your face. The same lunatic who has his teeth in everything?"

"-What the hell are you going to do here? You want me to kill you?"

I bring my hands to my mouth and blow a strong whistle. They both look at me amazed as frozen statues. Well, that's not really surprising. I whistled for Negar once and she was so amazed that I was scared that she might have a heart attack. It was as if she was paralyzed by my whistle; she just stood still and stared at me. She didn't speak to me for two days. I don't remember why I whistled at her. Now, these two dolls want to test me?

They want to keep going when the driver gets in and says, "Excuse me, pal, Can you use the back seat so this lady can sit in your place?"

I take a look at the woman who is wearing a milky manteaux and is wearing so much heavy make-up. She would pass for a woman in her thirties. She has her hands on her hips and is waiting for me to get out. I hesitate, but go behind anyway. The girl with the sunglasses is now next to me. She puffs and says: "Look who's sitting here, Yuck!" turning her back to me.

She turns her head towards her girlfriend. The driver wipes the sweat on her face with the silk handkerchief round his neck and checks everything in the mirror. Then she begins to talk to the same woman in the milky manteaux.

"-Any news from your wife and kids?"

"-They're not bad. They send their regards. But you don't know how this kid is giving us a bad time. I ask him what is eating you, you chump? You didn't do military service and we said OK. You said you needed a job and we rented a supermarket for you and filled it with things for sale and you sold everything and said nothing of it. Well, was there anything that we didn't do for you? I have no idea what we are supposed to do with this son-of-a-bitch. All there is on his mind is wasting time. Morning and night, he wastes his time with his pals. Now, he is telling his mother to find him a good girl maybe he could come to his senses. I'm scared really. It is bad times."

The woman nods to him and asks: "Does he have anyone on his mind?"

"-I told you, this idiot doesn't want to be stopped to find one, so That's what we plan to do for him."

"-Do you want a white and fat chick?" She asks.

I am surprised and my eyes are about to jump out. I wonder whether they're talking about selling cattle and sheep or the future of a boy and girl. Now is the time to go really mad and tell them: "No, ma'am! The guys are into sun-tanned and dark-skinned girls. Do they come in other colors too?" Maybe I'd like to be a prospective customer too. Or ask her whether she's trying to fix a girl for the cab driver when she is talking in that line?

"-Ow, this damn traffic! Who's this girl anyway?" She askes.

"-It's the daughter of one of our neighbors. She's a nice doll. I almost know her and her family. I would make a proposal if you like me to." She elaborates.

"-God bless you, sister! I'll talk to my wife tonight. I'll let you know later. Now, if you could spot a few girls for us and check them out to see which one is better, that would be just fine." He continues.

I get off a few blocks further. I am sweating. I don't know if it is because of the hot weather in May or because of them babbling. I see Babu close to the street. He's sitting and as always he has a pair of scales in front of him. Amir, the fruit-seller, who's a few feet away from him, throws some rotten fruit at him and says: "Whew, Babu, you chump! Eat it,

Babu, Hey! I'm talking to you, you little dog, why don't you eat it?"

Babu looks at him, but pays no attention. All the boys in the neighborhood call him 'Babu' because of his round head, fleshy ears and camel lips. A classical fool who is harmless. I have seen the sellers make fun of him many times, or some kids give him a kick or a slap when they walk around him. He makes a run for it with red eyes because he was scared. I have never seen him swear at anyone although everyone mistreats him. I once had had an argument with the guys and the sellers who mistreated him, but it was useless. They challenged me: "Who are you to take his side?"

A few times, after I saw my weight on his scales and paid him, he said: "Thank you very much. Thank you. Come back tomorrow. I'll be cheap."

Then, drooling, he laughed, and I liked the smile that came to his round face.

Although I know it is useless, I cannot help but say something again this time. Like Negar says, I should stop picking on others. I should just go to the fruit-seller and say: "Dear, sir, why are you annoying him?"

"-It's you again? Mind your own business."

"-What's this 'you again'? What's my 'business'?"

"-What it means is 'are you the police or the sheriff in this neighborhood'?"

"-I'm saying is for your own sake. What you do will have bad consequences." I explain.

"-Go mind your business. I'm not supposed to take lessons from no-good teachers like you."

I look at the tattoo on his arm. It is a tattoo of a pot and a written under it "we have seen the image of the beloved in the pot."

I chuckle and start to return to Babu.

As I do, Amir the fruit-seller asks: "What are you laughing about, you dummy?"

I turn to him blow a whistle at him. His mouth opens and he just stares at me. He wants to say something, but it is as if his mouth is locked. This kind of move can lock anyone up when it comes from a polite-looking teacher. Today, I don't know why, I'm into blowing whistles.

I return to Babu, who stretches out his hand and we shake a victory handshake.

"-Come, here, I'll be cheap."

Although I already know my weight, just to make him happy, I step onto the scales. He looks and announces: "Seventy. Seventy kilos. No, it's not seventy yet. Yes, it is now. It is now."

I give him some coins and he says: "Thank you. Come again, I'll be cheap."

As I go up the stairs, it's so quiet. I feel like blowing a whistle again. "But for whom this time? I wonder, perhaps I can do it for me, because I turned off the two girls and Amir." I smile.

It would be better to low my loud whistle here where nobody could see, as I stand, bring my hands to my mouth and make an ear-piercing whistle. The sound echoes throughout the corridor and I laugh about it. I want to do it again, but just as I bring my hands up to my mouth, a door opens, and move on at once.

"-I'm in the kitchen."

"-Aren't you ready yet?"

"-Yes, wait."

Negar comes into the room to change her dress. She looks at me in that special way, I give her a look and shake my head. "Well?" She asks.

"-Well what?"

"-Haven't you forgotten something?" she counters.

-I think for a moment: "We agreed on the chips and snacks and ice-cream in the park."

"-Then, you have forgotten it."

"-What? The green manteaux?"

She touches her lips and I realize that I haven't kissed her so I go to her and give her a kiss.

Nastaran interjects: "Then, you convinced Negar that you haven't cheated on her after all?"

"-I didn't make anyone believe that. I haven't cheated. Did I lie?"

"-So, who was this caller?"

"-I don't know."

"-You didn't think that it could be me?"

I chuckle: "You don't even exist."

"-But you are having an affair. Just the fact that you're thinking about me means having an affair. Come to think of it, are you cheating on me too? I know you're not the type, but sometimes guys do things that cannot be expected from them. Now, is there someone else?"

"-Leave me alone, for God's sake. How long are you going to say the same nonsense?"

"-What makes you sure that Negar has believed your word? I'm sure she has said to herself 'I'd wait to catch him red-handed and then I'll have a ball.'"

"-No way. Negar doesn't let these stupid ideas in her head like you do. Get lost. You're bothering me." I say dismissively.

"-I don't want to bother you. But you're the one who won't let me go. You ask me to go and I go. Then you call me back again. I have nothing to do with you. But you're insane and have no idea what you're doing. How long is this game going to go on?" she taunts.

"-I don't know. I think it's time to get rid of you."

"-It will be my pleasure. I wish you could get results. By the way, can I ask something?"

"-You'll get me mad if it's irrelevant."

"-Sure. Do you think Negar has someone else on her mind, just like you and me, and just like you she is resisting any confession that you're having an affair?"

"-Kindly shut up!"

"-Well, it was just a question."

"-Why are you always asking questions that shake my nerves?"

"-See, then, it's all clear, you do believe everyone might have someone like me?"

"-I didn't mean. Now, let's say Negar has someone for herself like I do; so, what?" I challenge back.

"-Don't feel any guilt for being with me. We can go on like this." She cajoles.

"-I don't want to! You must get out of my life. Do you understand? My life must be only for Negar. That's it. Shut up!"

"-Ok, I'll go for now, but know that I will make a mess of your life. I'm not going to back away just like that. You wait and see."

5

We move to the park. Since this morning, my mind has been occupied with that familiar voice; and I want to know who it was. I don't tell Negar anything about it because she would not let it go if I told her, and would shake my nerves with her questions.

When we come to the end of the alley, we see a crowd. Negar asks: if it is a fight?

We step forward to see. They are talking about Babu. Lord knows what they have done to him this time. One of the pals from the neighborhood sees me, so I ask, "What's up?"

"-Babu has hurt the fruit-seller."

"-Babu? How? Why?"

"-Amir kept annoying him untill Babu got wild, went behind him and hit him on the head with his scales. You can't imagine how bad it was bleeding."And points to the ground. "See how much blood there is".

"-It was his own fault. Babu never harmed anybody."

"-I know that and I saw you quarreling with Amir about Babu. I also told him a few times too that he must not annoy him. He didn't listen to me and that's what happened to him after all."

"-Now what has happened? Where has Babu gone?" I ask.

"-Amir was knocked down and they took him to hospital. Babu got away, he explained.

I take Negar's hand and we keep walking. Negar asks; "Has Amir, the fruit-seller ever hit Babu on the head?"

"-You were here when the pal was talking about it. Where's your head then?" I snap back.

"-Ahh, I just had a question and this is how you answer me," she exclaims defensively.

"-No, Amir didn't hit Babu. Babu hit Amir, with his pair of scales." I impatiently explain.

"-No way! I can't believe it. The boy wouldn't hurt a fly. Why were you arguing with Amir? You want to start a quarrel with the fruit-seller too? I asked you a hundred times not to start a quarrel."

I am silent. It is a good thing that I have not said anything about my quarrel with the two girls, or she would get really mad. Then, going to the park would be a very bitter experience for us.

We continue to walk to the park. I am both happy and sad. I'm happy that Babu moved a muscle at last yet I'm sad that he caused this event. What if something happens to Amir? What if Amir decides to sue him? Seeing the blood on the ground, one can guess it was a very hard blow. All there is on my mind is what will happen to Babu.

We enter the park and Negar talks like a baby: "Me chips". "Me snacks". "Me ice-cream."

We head for the buffet in the park; I get her everything that she wants and she swallows the snacks as if she hasn't had anything to eat in years. I eat too.

"-Any news from school?" she asks

"-Nothing unusual. What about you? You didn't get any prank call today, did you? Did you turn your cell phone off?"

"-No, I didn't, but nobody called either. How about you?"

"-She called me, but I scared her and she didn't call again." I explain.

"-What did you say to scare her?" she wants to know.

"-I said 'if you call again, I'll have someone trace you and then I'll sue you'."

"-Then do it. Why are you waiting for?" she demanded.

"-Come on. I'm not in the mood to go to a court and all that stuff. Let's see if she calls again. You can't lodge a complaint for no reason."

Although I am saying these things to Negar, I like to keep track of the story myself to see what it comes to. This is not something to be forgotten so easily, especially the familiar voice that I heard.

A young couple that are perhaps in their twenties pass by us holding each other's hands. The girl says: "I told mom that we are friends. I showed her a photo of you."

"Why did you do this? What did she say?" The boy asks.

"-Nothing. She said we have to wait and see," and lowers her head slightly.

The boy seems to be upset that the girl had told her mother about them. Negar quickly asks: "Did you see it? Did you see that the boy was upset?"

"-I guess so," trying to be nonchalant. Now only few feet away from us, they are standing face to face and are arguing.

" What do you think happened?" Negar asks. "They were so good to each other."

"-I can only guess: "the boy is upset that her mom knows about them."

"-Why?" Negar

I stare into her eyes; "because boys don't think about getting married at his age and they want to spend time with girlfriends and have fun with them."

"-What a powerful psychologist! How confident of you, Mr. Teacher. You learned so much about them by a couple of words that heard from their lips?" Negar chides

"-Sorry. It is my opinion, just an opinion. That's it. My mistake. Forgive me."

The girl suddenly walks out of the park and the boy passes by us just as another boy appears from behind the trees and asks him, "What happened? What were you arguing about?"

"Forget it. The girl is crazy. She thinks I want to marry her." He explains."

The other boy exclaims, "You shouldn't have left her. She was really something!"

"-I'll find another one. There are so many girls. They grow like the grass in the park."

They move away and Negar is surprised and gives me a look. It seems you know a thing or two."

"-I don't know; I only pay some attention. Can you guess what happens now?"

"-No."

"-The girl who just walked out goes home and sits in a corner to write her whole life story and talk about the boys who think girls are like the grass in the park and then mails it to your magazine." I snicker.

"-Please god, release me from this lunatic! You're just waiting for something to happen to find faults with our magazine. Forget it, for god's sake!"

She has eaten all the snacks and she's now going for the chips. I wait for her to finish her chips and when she is done, she cleans her mouth and continues: Ok, now, let's go to the park's gallery. I have heard some photography works are on display."

This is understood. The first photo shows an old man wearing a shabby coat and standing in the rain with only a piece of nylon on his head. One can tell from the way he's standing that he's trembling.

The second shows a mother on the sidewalk and a young girl, maybe ten or eleven years old, has laid her head on her lap. The mother is stretching her empty hand out to the people who pass by.

The third photo depicts a child with a pack of zodiac cards in his hand and a thumb in his mouth. He is staring at the camera lens.

The fourth is of a man lying on his belly on the sidewalk and from the coins around him and his pale face, one can tell he is dead.

I am so obsessed with viewing the photos that I suddenly bump into somebody, and immediately say; "I am so sorry."

I don't look at his face, just pass by.

"-I would have still loved you even if you had not apologized."

Negar is so surprised and I turn back to the voice. I look at him, then almost close my eyes and, in an instant, we hug each other. I did not believe that my friend with his stylish hair has gone bald after two years since the last time I saw him. I couldn't recognize him at first sight. Negar is standing , watching us with a smile. I quickly introduce

Soroush to her and we go and sit in a café and order sour cherry sorbet. Once settled Soroush asks; "Well, dear friend! How's everything? You got married and forgot all of us".

"-Soroush, dear, let's say I got married and did forget you, then, why is it that you forget all about me? What's that look on you face? What happened to your lady-killer hair?" I chide

"-My hair was gone with the storm." He declares his hand gently over his new bald head.

"-Any news from college? Have you finished it or not?" I ask

He makes a deep sigh and says; "I finished my Master's degree."

"-Good for you! What stamina! You even left me behind." I am genuinely happy for him.

"-It was no good though." He laments.

"-Why so hopeless? You must be very active now."

"-You have no idea. I got my degree yet I don't have a job. I can't get a job anywhere and they don't let me have any kind of activity. I have written some plays, but didn't get the permission to have them published or put them on a stage. This is how things are. I am being condemned to be jobless because I only write according to my own will and taste."

"-Then, how do you make ends meet?"

He shrugs and says: "This is a secret. A big secret."

"-Is it so big that you can't tell me?"

-Negar says interjects: "Maybe, Soroush is not comfortable to say it while I'm here."

"-No, lady, it's not that, you think wrong, I better tell you. I don't want you to get upset. But promise not to tell anybody," Soroush quickly corrects

"We promise," Negar and I say in

"-I work with one of my pals. On the street," he confesses

"-On the street. What kind of work?" we

"-We sing and play instruments. One day, my pal plays the accordion and I become the blind man wearing dark glasses with a bowl in hand. We go up and down the Valiasr Street. If there is a celebration; I paint my face black and sing a song. And if there is a mourning; I wear black and perform passion plays on the street in such a way that no one can recognize me..." his voice trails off.

"-Stop being funny!" I command incredulously.

"-Take it from me. This is no joke. It's the truth."

"-You must be joking. That's nonsense."

He looks down and says; "You can think however you like."

"-Now, let's say, you do this, how much can you get? What can you do it with the money?" I now ask, genuinely concerned.

"-Well, if you promise not to compete with me, I tell you I get twice the money you get as a teacher," raising his head and his voice

Negar looks at us without saying anything and perhaps like me she thinks she's hearing all this in a dream. I frown and breathe in and out with anger. Soroush realizes that I am angry and continues: "I told you it's not as bad as you think."

"-Do me a favor and say nothing more."

Negar bites her lips trying to tell me that I must more polite.

"-I remember you used to say that the important thing is not to come to a blind alley in life, that I should always have to find a way outs or make one. Today, if I have these blind alleys in front of me, that's how I find a way out of them."

I smile and say; "What an interesting use by my words. You think you'll get anywhere?"

"-I'm getting somewhere. I collected some money doing this job and I'm leaving for France. The Westerners, while they are so cold in life and relationships, have so many passions for art and respect it. I'll go there. It is important to spend my art somewhere, whether it is here or France," he says confidently.

We are sit in silence for a couple of moments. Soroush finishes the sour cherry sorbet in an instant and suddenly gets up ; "Excuse me. I have to see someone. It was nice seeing you. I hope I'll see you again," extending his hand. I press his hand firmly. "Call me if you have time so we can be together. If you decide to go abroad anytime soon, let me know."

He says goodbye and leaves. Negar takes my hand and lifts me. I cannot find any words. Negar knows this and tries to make me speak.

"-I can't believe it. Why should they do that?" she finally asks.

I don't answer. I have no answer. We walk to the middle of the park. A stone buffalo is place in the middle. Hoping for a distraction Negar says: "I like it very much. Look. It's in one piece. How did they make this?"

"-I don't know. But it's an interesting work." I reply hay-heartedly.

"-How strange! There's finally something you actually like and you're saying 'I don't know'. That's a breakthrough."

"-Well, I don't really know. Is that a crime?"

"-No. but it's the first time you have given me this answer."

"-Oh, so knowing something is a crime then." I challenge back.

She frowns and looks away.

"-You're depressed again? So, your friend has these problems, it has nothing to do with me, does it? Why aren't you speaking to me? We came to the park to have fun. I'm not here to look at your frowns."

"She touches the buffalo as if she is enjoying its soft skin. A small boy who has also approached the stone buffalo tells his mother: "Mommy, I want to ride on it."

"-This is not for a ride. It's put here so people can see it." She gently explains.

He kicks the ground and demands: "I want to! I want to!"

"-Honey, I can't lift you." coddling him softly.

I look at the mother and offer to give him a lift so he can have a ride on it.

She accepts so I lift the small boy so he can sit on the buffalo. They boy moves himself up and says: "Hurrah! go, go! See, Mommy! See I'm on it!"

"-I can see that! Bravo, my little boy." The mother is beaming now.

"I'm jealous. I wish I was that age and could have a ride too. I could transform into Zorro, or the Spiderman, or maybe Batman and Superman and see myself as a powerful man who can do everything. I wish everything was as simple as this little boy who asked for a ride on the buffalo."

"-We must go back home now; Come on, come down. Uncle Pourang is on TV now!" his mother

But it's not the time for the Uncle Pourang program! What a lying mom! Isn't telling a lie actually betraying a child?

The boy shakes his head as I bring him down. Negar looks at the boy and touches his cheeks. The mother says "Thank you" and they leave. Negar is still smiling about the sweet kid when I ask: would you like having a fat kid like that?

"-I like having one but you wouldn't accept it."

"-First, practice being a mom." I snap back

She murmurs something quietly and I cannot hear.

"-Say it loudly and let me hear it too. Who are you talking to?" I demand.

"-I'm talking to myself and it is rude of you to ask. Look, I want that green manteaux, no matter what." Now that's the one demanding.

"-What does it have to do with it? We were talking about having a baby."

"-We are only talking about the 'green manteaux' now."

"-I have no money."

"-Well for now, we can go and ask about price. If you are not coming along, I swear, I will start walking backwards."

That's how she childishly insists. Every time she asks for something and I say "no", she walks backwards to attracts the look of the others and makes me feel disgusted.

"-Do you want to know if I can make a fuss too?" I threaten.

"-What are you going to do?"

"I jump on to the stone buffalo and shout so loudly everyone can hear: "go", "go", I have become the Zorro! Everyone just look at me. I am Zorro!"

Negar covers her face with her hands in embarrassment and says: "Oh, gosh, come down. You're embarrassing me. What are you doing?"

A few young people standing a little further away laugh at me. One of them says: "Good for you, Zorro!"

Negar pulls me down the stone buffalo, but she can't help laughing. She hits me on my arm and says: "Then, look at me now!" and begins walking backwards. Everyone is laughing at us again. A girl shouts out: "What color is your pills, mister? Give us one or two. We are dying with sadness."

Negar twists her ankle and falls back when she turns to look at the girl and. I run to her. She's lying on her back and doesn't want to get up. I stretch my hands to her and say: "Get up. You are shameless."

"-I'm not getting up." She declares definitely ."-I want to go and ask about the manteaux. Are you coming?" As she takes my hand and gets up and taunts: You surrendered, didn't you?"

She has my hand and is pulling me along with her. Four policemen pass by and run to the center of the park towards just as youths, who had been sitting there without a care in the world begin to run away. They catch two of them and two more officers join them. They handcuff both of them and leave the park. I hear one of the boys saying: I have done nothing, I swear! I am just nobody."

One of the officers takes small packs out of his pocket, shows them and yells: "Have I made a mistake? Are you the wrong guy?"and gives him a kick and a slap on the back of his neck as they go away. We exit the park and walk to the square. We arrive at the Passage where they often sell manteaux and she shows me the one she wants in the window and says: "This is the one."

"-Negar, if it's expensive, you are the one paying for it, I am telling you."

We enter the store and I ask the salesman how much it is. When he answers, Negar herself realizes that it is much too expensive for us. I thank the salesman and we step out of the store. Negar is looking down silently.

She is depressed. I don't know why buying a manteaux means so much her that it changes her mood.

As we arrive home, we see a police car and an ambulance. There is a crowd too right in front of our condo. I guess they are here to take Babu, but surely they haven't sent several policemen just to take Babu, not to mention, he doesn't live in our neighborhood. We get closer with larger steps. A policeman stops us. I face the officers and say; "We live in this condo, officer. Is something wrong?"

He tells the other office to let us pass. Negar is so pale. As we go further. the officer asks: "Which flat is yours?"

"-We live on the third floor." We explain.

"-Then, you must know Mr. Shahi."

"-Yes. He's our neighbor. Has something happened?"

He leads us inside to the stairs and quietly states: "I'm afraid to tell you that Mr. Shahi has been murdered."

Negar is now trembling with fear: "What? Murdered? No, I'm not going up the stairs." and grabs my arm tightly. Then she loses heart and sits on the stairs. She's sick. The woman from our condo takes her hand and leads her to her apartment. The officer turns to me and says; "I hope you won't have a weak heart too because you must help us."

"-How can I help you?" I reply.

"-Just be relaxed and follow me," He commands.

As we go to the third floor. I am scared but I have to control myself. We stop at Mr. Shahi's door. The officer then asks my name and goes in. There are several people already in the apartment. He comes out and instructs me to: Come in. The Major wants to see you."

I takes shaky steps as I walk in. in the middle of the hall, is Mr. Shahi covered with a white sheet; there is blood all over the floor. There is a card on the dead body and it has 'number 1'written on it. I take my swallow hard and keep heady . I feel heavy. Murdered! is unbelievable to me.

One of the officers is still taking photos of the things inside the house and two people are taking the fingerprints.

The Major asks; "You live right in front of his flat. Is that right, Mr. Pakravan?"

"-Yes, I … my wife and I .

Why am I saying "my wife and I '? maybe I want to make him understand that I mind my own business. The major wearing a black suit shows no sign of stress and fear as he asks me this question and answer. Just looking at him makes one feel powerful: His tiny eyes are rather attractive in his fleshy eyelids; His face is clean shaven and one feels a good just watching him.

"-Have a seat, please." He instructs.

I sit facing him directly. He has some papers in his hand that I think belong to Mr. Shahi. He checks the back and front of the papers.

"-How well did you know him? Of course, what I mean is 'how well' and 'how close were you'?"

It is hard for me to speak. I murmur "Since a year ago, since I married my wife. We have been living in this apartment. I know Mr. Shahi since then. He had moved in a few months before that. Of course, we rent our cando. But, as far as I know, Mr. Shahi owned the house.

"-Well, tell me how you got to know Mr. Shahi and what was your involvement with him?" the major continues.

"-Involvement? Well, we were neighbors. The first time I saw him was the day we brought my wife's stuffs. He was a kind man. He knocked at our door and said he had made some tea for us and asked us to come to his apartment to have tea. Since that day, we were involved more or less. That's it."

Before I was able to add anything, he asks; "Excuse me, can I ask what your occupation ?"

"-I am a teacher."

"-Well, Mr. Pakravan! What you're saying doesn't help me. You must know him better than that because you knew him better than anyone else. So, please, tell us more."

I explain everything that I recall that was exchanged between Mr. Shahi and me. The poor guy was dead and I was nothing more than just his listener."

When I'm finished, he asks: "Can I ask where you were when he was murdered?"

-"What time was that?"

"-Two or three hours ago."

I don't like this question. They ask this question when you are a suspect.

"-My wife and I were in the park."

"-Park? Do you always go to the park with your wife?" he leans in.

"-When we need to," I explain

He shakes his head "When did you leave and did you notice anything when you were leaving?"

"-We left at 6 o'clock and didn't see anything."

"-Did anyone have a grudge against Mr. Shahi? Do you know about anything that can help us?" he asked, leaning in further

"-Mr. Shahi wasn't really talking to anyone so no one had a grudge against him. He didn't have anybody. He used to have a wife and a son in the past and they are now dead. That's it. No relatives or no acquaintance, and no nothing." I'm now nervously rambling

He continues "You just mentioned that he has a weblog. Can you show us his weblog, With his own computer that is still on?"

We go to the computer. Passing Mr.shahi dead body scares me a bit. By the way, why are we afraid of dead bodies? Isn't it that the soul has left the body and they don't make a move? Perhaps, we are afraid that the soul might return and the dead will come alive again.

"-Have the fingerprints been taken? If you're done, we have some work to do," the major directs an officer.

"Yes, sir, we are done."

"I sit down on Mr. Shahi's computer chair and show the major his weblog. Then I get up and he sits down. He through the topics, looks at me and says: "There is nothing you can do for us right now. Thank you for your cooperation. By the way, you are not allowed to leave the city and give your phone number to the officer."

"-Sorry, but my fingerprints could be on this too. Won't that be a problem for me?"

"-Don't be scared if you haven't done anything. It doesn't matter if your fingerprints can be found here."

"-Excuse me for asking, but who called you?" I asked as I was leaving.

"-What difference does that to you?" he counters.

"-I am just curious. That's all. Because we and Mr. Shahi live on the top floor and no one else comes here," I explain.

"-We don't know that yet. If you learn anything about this, be sure to call us."

He takes a card out of his pocket and gives it to me, but I'm looking at the corpse. I turn to the Major and ask; Can I see the body?"

He raises his eyebrows. Why? "For what?"

"-I want to see his face for the last time ,but only, if it's OK, of course"

"-You're not allowed to see the corpse. But, just for your information, there is no face anymore. The bullet was shot from the back and it has disfigured his face. It is a disgusting scene." He elaborates and returns to the computer screen.

I feel that I'm hollow. I cannot feel anything inside me; it is as if my heart has stopped. I remember Shahi saying; "Consider death as a person who is holding a pistol behind you, one that can blow your brains out whenever he wants."

6

Mr. Shahi is sitting in front of me with the electrical tool that changes his voice into the voice of a robot, I don't know what it is called. "So, you too believed that I am dead?"

But this time his voice isn't anything like that voice of a robot. It is the voice of a monster from a movie. His fingers are long like the fingers of Dracula with long and black nails.

"-Well, yeah, I believed it," I answer.

"-Did you see the body too?"

"-Yes. No, there was a white sheet on it."

"-You didn't see it because they didn't allow you. Is that right?"

"-Yes, that's right. But how do you know that?"

"-It's always like that. We give our opinions without seeing the details." He explains.

"-Now, are you here to give me your philosophical views? I ask impatiently" "I was about to freeze to death and Negar looked pale as a corpse. What kind of sick joke is that?"

He stares at me. His eyes suddenly turn into two bowls of blood. I am frightened; I don't see well; I'm so scared that I cannot breathe well.

"-I am here to sing a song for you; do you like it?"

"I have to grin: "It's no time for such things, is it? What has happened here, Mr. Shahi?"

He puts the electrical tool to his mouth like a microphone as if performing on stage, then stands and looks around the room: "Listen everybody. I want to sing a song for you."

I can hear whistles and claps and a lot of noises. It is like being in a concert. Then whole room becomes dark and a circle of light falls on Mr. Shahi; he sings. His voice is now like that of a young man. He suddenly pauses for a few instants and his tears now begin flowing like blood. Now Like a cassette stuck in the stereo, his voice is no longer clear.

A man in black appears in the back with a pistol in his hand and before I can say anything puts the gun to Mr.Shahi head and shoots. His brain splatter all overme. I shout and boost up in my bed and my whole body is covered with sweat. The house is as quiet as a graveyard and Negar isn't here either. I remember sent her to her mother's house. It was better for her not to be here tonight. I was afraid she might lose her mind with fear but I still prefer to stay in my own house, even though just a few meters from my house someone has been murdered. I turn on the light. It's three o'clock in the morning. I breathe with difficulty. Finally I decide to go to the bath to take a shower hoping to feel better. When I come out, I drink a glass of fruit juice and feel better so I go back to bed. But I don't feel sleepy. So I get up and get Shamlu's book of poetry. I open the book and begin to read. A poem appears before my eyes and I had once heard Farhad (the popular singer) sing when I was in Mr. Shahi's place. Quietly I try to sing the same way it sounded.

A moonlight night

Moon comes to my dreams

Takes me to the end of the road

Where its nights, one and lonely

The single elm tree

Happy and cheerful

Stretches its hand

To let a star drop like a raindrop

My eyes are now heavy, but I'm still immersed in the book when Nastaran comes and lies on the bed beside me. She is wearing Negar's silk dress. I don't mind her and keep on singing; and she sings alonger with me.

One night after all

Moon comes to all

Over this hill

Moon starts to smile

One night comes the moon

One night comes the moon

When we come to the end of the poem and Nastaran gives me a clap. Her claps echo in the room. I grit my teeth but I still don't say a word; I read another poem. She grabs the book and tosses it away, puts her head on my chest, and says: "Your heart is beating 'Nastaran, Nastaran'."

"-No, this heart is now beating 'Negar, Negar'."

"-What's the world coming to if it says 'Nastaran' for one night?"

I annoyed, I stands up and shout: "No! This damn heart of mine must not say your name anymore! It must only say 'Negar, Negar'. That's it. Damn you! Why don't you leave me alone. Get lost, you piece of trash. Go away and don't come back. I remember you broke up with me and said you'd make a mess of my life. So what now? Why couldn't you do a damn thing?" I am angry now

"Ok, I'll go forever. But I said I would make your life a mess first and then I would disappear. Wait and see!" the storms back.

"-You won't do a damn thing. You are nothing. Nothing! Now, get out of my sight."

"-You will see what I can do to you. I will make you helpless. You think I don't exist? No, mister, I am the sheer truth that you think is imaginary."

I now shout with all my strength: "Shut up! Shut up! Shut up!"

Suddenly a hand is shaking me. I open my eyes and see Negar is sitting on the bed beside me saying: "Wake up. You're dreaming."

Now I am breathing sharply and sweating. I look at the clock. It's almost 12 o'clock noon and I have been having strange dreams since I went into bed last night. Nastaran doesn't leave my head either. She continually bothers me and I don't know what I should do, but I have to think of something after all.

"-How did you get here? Wasn't I supposed to pick you up?" I ask, still feeling danger.

"-Nazanin drove me here. We were awakened by her neighbors early this morning."

-"Why what was the matter?" I ask.

-" The neighbor's son had hanged himself."

"I chuckle. "How odd. This one is killed, that one kills himself. Babu hits the fruit-seller in the head. The girl with the letter turns out to be a murderer. Sheila becomes a hooker. Mastaneh has an abortion. And it is the destiny of my pal with a Master's degree in theatrical fiction to paint himself black and amuse people in the street for a little money. This is called a safe and quiet society?" I exclaim

"-What a blissful morning! when you start the day with these complaints it will surely have a beautiful end."

I now can hear Nazanin's voice in another room: "The poor boy had a fiancée and was a college student. I knew the fiancée. We went to the same school. They had been engaged for a couple of years, but the boy didn't have the money to get married. He didn't have a job either and couldn't pay the college fees. Her father said that there would be no marriage if he couldn't get married by the end of spring."

"well that's a good story, yes? I say to Negar" "You can print it in your magazine and will get lots of readers. The story has marriage, love, poverty, unemployment, and traditional families .everything in it…"

She puts her hand on my mouth and pushes me back on the bed. "Go to sleep, honey. You're not feeling well now. You have gotten up on the wrong side of the bed today. Now tell me. Who were you telling to shut up in you dream?"

"-You." I lie.

"-Why?"

"-You were nagging about the green manteaux and trying to talk me into buying it so I was saying 'shut up'."

She grabs the pillow and hits me on the side and goes out of the room. I slowly get up and go to the kitchen where Negar and Nazanin are.

"-I'm starving." I announce, trying to sound normal.

"-Hello."

"-Hello, Miss Nazanin. I'm starving."

" Wait till we have lunch together. It's not time for breakfast now." Negar . "What was with Mr. Shahi yesterday?"

"-He died." He was murdered.

-I know that, you funny boy, but Who did it?

"-Nobody knows; I was thinking about Shahi all night and I was having nightmares. Let me forget about him. I'm begging you." I pleaded.

"-I'm really going crazy. I can't believe it. I feel sorry for him. Do his relatives know about it? Didn't anyone else come to ask questions about him?" she continued.

-Perhaps there was money or jewelry in the house and someone who knew had...

"-No. Nothing was touched in the house. Even the money that could be seen was not taken. One who comes in with a gun like that to kill must be a professional. Blowing his brains out isn't something that everybody can do. It can't be the work of an ordinary murderer either." I explain.

"Poor soul. I saw him once. He was a quiet man."

I must change the subject, but They don't let it go like that, so I say; "Well, Nazanin, tell us about the boy."

"Although his story isn't less tragic than that of Shahi, it is the story of a stranger and I feel less pity for him. We only talk about everyday bitter events. Does anything sweet happen which we can speak about?"

"Nothing else, says Nazanin. It was all I said. These things are normal nowadays. Just this year, four students in our college killed themselves."

"-Is that true? Why?"

"-For many reasons. One of them was a girl who looked very innocent."

"-So, why did this so-called innocent girl decide to kill herself?"

"-I have no idea."

down and she say; "You won't believe how this girl killed herself."

"-Tell me if it's interesting."

"-We were dismissed, and were walking out of our faculty; when without any screams or yells; a girl suddenly lands in the yard. Can you imagine? No you can't; you can't imagine the splashed brains of a person who has landed on the ground from the seventh floor. It was like a dream."

When I look at her carefully, I can see a thin layor of tears in her eyes. Negar understands it and says; "Oh, you two have nothing to talk about except 'death'?"

"-I'm waiting for lunch." I remind them.

"-All right. I'll call you when the lunch is ready."

The face of Nastaran is still before my eyes, so I quietly say; "Shut up. Shut up."

I go to my small library to pick a book to read until the lunch is ready. Once more, I remember the familiar voice which said "hang up". And it sounded a lot like Nazanin. I am not wrong. "Does it mean...no...Nazanin wouldn't try to make her sister's life...but she sounded like her. Damn it. Why can't I recognize that voice?"

The doorbell rings. I shout: "Get the door. I'm busy."

"-Yes. What do you want? Yes, he is here. Who are you? Wait a minute."

Nazanin enters in my room. Arman, a lady named Nastaran wants to speak to you."

I am speechless and can't breathe. I stare at Nazanin; finally find my voice and ask: Who wants to speak?"

"-Nastaran. Why are you asking like this? Is something wrong?"

"I had never experienced the freezing of my soul in a second. This is the first time. Nastaran, Nastaran, Nstaran. How can it be? God, am I dreaming? But I'm awake now. But what does 'Nastaran' mean? Does it mean that an imaginary person is now real and has come to make a mess of my life and then vanish. Is she now at the door? I go to the window. "Perhaps, this is only a woman whose name is also 'Nastaran'. That's it. Don't lose your mind. Maybe this is a game too. I look below the window. Oh God! What is this! How close is reality to imagination? That's Nastaran herself! She's wearing an apri of sunglasses and a bunch of flowers. How hard is it for someone to choose laughter, then scream, and shout to empty oneself?"

"Why don't you go to see her?" Negar asks. "The poor girl is waiting. Now, who is this Nastaran?" I do not answer.

I run to the door, open it and look at her again. There she is. It's Nastaran. I scratched my hand while I was going down and suddenly feel the pain and know that I'm awake. I am awake. It's Nastaran. She looks at me and laughs: "Hi. Didn't I tell you I would come to see you one day, no matter where you are? It seems that you can't believe that it's me."

Nastaran, Negar, Nazanin and I. We all sitting at the table to have lunch. A silence whose weight I can feel on my heart fills the entire house. Negar inspects every move Nazanin makes in a way that she cannot notice. Seeing Nastaran was as unbelievable to me as seeing the sun at night.

When I first saw her at the door, I demanded: "What are you doing here?"

On the one hand, seeing the Nastaran, who I was in love with at a time excited me but on the other hand I feel fear seeing the imaginary 'Nastaran' who wants to get me into trouble. But it's not only that she is not imaginary, though the imaginary 'Nastaran' is a wave of my love for this 'Nastaran'. "You know she is imaginary, then, why are you so scared?" the voice in my head asked. The real one left me yet her image stayed with me. For three years, she hasn't left me and here she is now. But this time, it's for real. She has appeared so unexpectedly that I suspect she might be the fictional one trying to shake everything in my life. Was the prank call from her? But, no, this 'Nastaran' wouldn't do such things. That 'Nastaran' is an imagination too. "What the hell are you saying? If you review what you have been saying to yourself, then you know that you are delirious. You're insane. Pull yourself together. It's just a friendly visit. That's all."

"Thank God! I always thought you have it in you to pick a good wife for yourself. She's made an excellent dish and she looks pretty too." Nastaran compliments.

Negar hadn't smiled since Nastaran come in but is now smiling! and returns the complement: "You're so kind. Of course, my husband has told me that he had classy and pretty friends like you."

"As Arman always says; we're all insane and those of us who have studied literature can better hide our insanity."

Only to say something, Nazanin also asks: "Where are you from?"

Nastaran turns her head and replies; "I am from the heart, darling."

The way she talks, moves, laughs and looks is still the same as before, and she excites even the strangers that see her for the first time. We laugh, all of us, and every moment that passes my heart loses some weight. I must have a word too.

"-When she says 'I am from the heart', she is right as someone who knows Shahnameh and the poems of Hafiz by heart. One who excels the naughty college professors in analyzing the poems of Molavi can only be from the heart."

"-It's kind of you, dear friend. You've always been my luminary. You gave me fresh life. You introduced me to myself and only then I could know what life means?"

"So what do you think life means?" Nazanin asks.

"-Life means life."

"-That's it?"

"-Yes, that's it. But you can't come to sense the meaning of 'life is life' so easily. She continues.

Nazanin shrugs and looks at me. I am still thinking that familiar voice could have been Nazanin's voice. So I have to play a trick to see if it was her at the right time.

Nazanin continues: When I met Arman, I realized what life means. I was a selfish person and Arman gave me a hard time when I was seeing him. So, Arman, do you still have the habit of saying 'Idiot, fool, stupid'? Haven't you learned anything new?"

Negar laughs, "You mean, you know about that too?"

"-At first, when got so mad at each other, I called me a 'female ass' and I called him the 'jack ass'."

Neagr and Nazanin laugh loudly while I just keep looking at Nastaran without reaction.

"-I'm sorry, Arman. I just wanted to catch up on old times. That's all." Nazanin adds

"-It's no problem. If we didn't use the word 'ass' to call each other, maybe, we could never realize what an asses we are. Just knowing that we were wrong and had to pick the right path was great."

Nastaran adds: "I was a real fool. Selfish and moody. But Arman was just being himself."

"What do you mean by that?" Negar wants to know.

"-I mean he had known himself. He had no childish concerns. He was always a few steps ahead of the other college boys and girls and many were jealous of him for that. But he had a major problem. He complained about everything, but most of the time he was after 'theology'."

Then she turns to me, shakes her head and says; "He got many kicks and punches from the guys whose religious bluffs were overwhelming!"

Negar puts down the spoon. "He was kicked and punched? For what?"

"We had some classmates who seemed to be too religious and had many awful claims about theology. They said absurd things and Arman made fun of them and said they were superstitious. So, they tried to outsmart him and they always failed. In one of the free discussion sessions, Arman made them appear as fools and everybody gave him a big clap."

"From that day on, Nastaran fell in love with me, but it was not a love that could make a good marriage. She loved my way of thinking. A couple of days later, after that session, some guys jumped out of a car on the street and assaulted me. I was in hospital for three days. The scar on my shoulder is from that day. I don't know how those bastards were hitting me and the scar is still there."

-With concern Nastaran asks; "You still have it on your shoulder?"

I freeze up, feel the blood circulation has slowed in my veins. I feel the way Negar is looking at me. "Is she thinking that an old affair is coming into sight? I'm afraid what the fictional 'Nastaran' had told me might be right. She said; 'Negar is just staying with you to find symptoms of your affair and she will deal with you when she finds them."

"It's still there." I confirm. "I think it'll stay until the end of my life like tattoo."

Nastaran then turns to Negar and explains: It was an awful wound. He called me from the hospital and asked me to bring him some money. He didn't call his family and didn't go home till he was all right again. I still feel bad whenever I remember the stitches on his shoulder. It was that time,that I knew how much I loved Arman."

I panic: "oh, God, what is this fool saying?" I want to stand up and yell at her and ask whether she is the fictional or real Nastaran.

"-She goes on: your husband was like a brother to me. In this strange city, I could always count on your husband. He was the only person who could be trusted. All the other boys were playing stupid games but Arman wasn't like them. There was only him and his God. I still love him like a brother."

I release the air that has been locked up in my chest for some time, and feel relaxed that things haven't got worse. I am happy to see that she knows how to speak and express her love."Now, we are in the sitting room and I'm happy to see that Nazanin and Negar have gotten used to her and now they are more interested in speaking to her than I am. But Nastaran suddenly changes the subject. "Well, dear friends! It was a good time!"opens her purse and takes out a gift and hands it to me.

"-This is a friendly gift for my college friend. Now you must excuse me if I bothered you. Negar, dear, thank you for the lunch. I didn't come to stay. You were so nice. I hope I can make it up to you."

"Don't say that. It was a pleasure," Negar

"-Well I must be on my way now. I'm leaving. I'm leaving Iran, but I couldn't bring myself to go without saying goodbye to Arman."

"-Are you going on your own? Where?"

"-No, I'm leaving with my husband. Somewhere very far. What difference does it make. It would be better if you didn't know.

Negar pleads: "Stay a little longer. You've just come. We were just beginning to have a good time."

"-No, I must be going now. I'm supposed to take my husband sight-seeing in Tehran. He is not from here and now that we're going abroad, he said that we should see Tehran first and then leave."

I am completely lethargic but I don't know why? "Why? You don't know why? Perhaps because you like her to be always there for you. You love both her presence and her soul. She is going to experience another world. She's leaving with another man. You will be left with only the imaginary 'Nastaran'. What will you going to do now? What will you do to 'Nastaran'? Can you take a knife and press it in her heart? No, you can't. Nastaran is leaving and she may or may not come here again. But, it has nothing to do with you, does it?"

"-Well, dear friend. Any last words?" she asks as she turns to me

"-Arman, Nastaran is asking you."

I come to my senses. "You're leaving so soon? Stay a little longer."

"-No, I said I must be going now," she asserts.

"-As you wish , but don't forget us wherever you go."

"-I called your number but you were never available. I called home and got your address from your mother. I know you don't have my new number. Of course, I'll need a new number after leaving Iran, so I can't give you this number. Then, I'll call you when I get there a number so we can stay in touch. After all, abroad is always 'abroad'. It doesn't matter whether you're in Paris or New York."

Foolishly, I repeat what I said a few moments ago and say: You're leaving so soon? Stay a little longer."

I once heard a beautiful sentence: "when words become worthless in one's mind, one spends them aimlessly." Now that she's leaving, everything will become worthless to me. When she goes away, many of the words will become useless in my mind. She repeats her answer: "No, I said I must be going."

I say it again: "As you wish. Don't forget us wherever you go."

But what do I desire? I want her to stay. Damn it! I know after she's gone, I'll never believe she was here. It will be like a dream and only some vague images will remain in my head. "You can keep her busy to stay longer. You know how to do it, why don't you try? Why don't you bring the book of Hafiz poetry and ask her to recite some verses? Why didn't you speak about Shamlu and Golestan? This way, you would have had different opinions and had to argue for hours. Maybe you're thinking that it is better to let her go. So much the better if she went away, but what would be better this way?" Nobody knows how I feel; three years, I've been having a hard time. My body goes to see her off but I see my soul squatting in a corner of my room; touched and caressed by the imaginary

'Nastaran'. She goes, she goes, she goes. And now she's gone and I'm left here. I close the door and go back. Negar and Nazanin are doing the dishes in the kitchen. My soul is still squatting in that corner, and now Nastaran is crying for him too. I feel I have turned into a rock that will have to view this corner of my room forever.

I open my eyes. It's dark everywhere. Am I dreaming again? I look around to see if Mr. Shahi is sitting somewhere around me and wants to sing for me. I rub my face. I can't believe it's night. Since Nastaran has left me, I decide to try to sleep to forget about her left.

I get up, hear the television noise and go out of the room. Nazanin is sitting behind the computer and surfing the net. Negar sees me and says: "Did you sleep well? What happened? You just passed out. I called you but you didn't move."

"-I told you I didn't sleep well last night."

"-But you woke up at 12 o'clock."

I hear the doorbell again. I am startled. I am afraid it's Nastaran again. But why should I be afraid? I sincerely hope they will not be Negar's parents coming to stay. I can't stand the sight of any visitor now. They are not in the habit of calling first. I go and open the door. It's the Major who asked me questions about Mr. Shahi yesterday morning.

"-Hello. Can I take your time for a few minutes?"

"-Sure. Come in."

He comes inside and sits on the sofa, looks around. Negar and Nazanin are busy in the kitchen.

"-Do you have guests?" he asks

"- Not really. It's my sister-in-law. I'm at your service." I answer him

"- Yes. As I told you, Mr. Shahi has been shot with a pistol from the behind. The bullet has been fired close to the body and has disfigured the victim's face. Nothing has been stolen from the house. I wanted to know more about you and Mr. Shahi." He said looking over his glasses.

I remain silent for a few moments. He doesn't expect me to start talking right away; he knows his job well. His grey hair and his look show him to be an experienced man. His look seeming to read my mind. I'm a little nervous, but I need to control myself. I don't know why I think I am the prime suspect.

"-I don't anything more to add to what I said before. Mr. Shahi was a lone wolf. During the last year, I didn't see anyone paying him a visit. During the hours that we spent together, his telephone didn't ring once. I never knew how he makes ends meet. I thought he was retired and was a pensioner. That's it. He was using the internet all the time."

"-Why didn't you ask how he made ends meet?" he queried.

"-I did ask him, and I asked him many other questions but he didn't give straight answers. He only spoke about things he liked." I continued.

"What did he search for on the internet?"

"-Nothing in particular. I told you that he was web logger and wrote his ideas on his weblog and was in contact with his audience. He sometimes wrote political or philosophical texts. Just that . He didn't call or meet anyone, but he sometimes chatted with them on the internet. Of course, that's all I know. He often talked to me about the discussions he had with others."

"-But, it is possible that he left something out." The major pressed on.

"- Maybe so."

"-Did he have a grudge against anyone in the neighborhood? Or anyone else?"

"- No. He held to himself, like I said."

"-Did you have a difference of opinion." His eyes now piercing straight at me.

"- On what?"

"-The things he said or wrote," directing back quickly.

"-I didn't agree on some of the things he wrote. But I didn't argue with him. I only gave him some credit. That man needed just that. I didn't want to argue with him and bother him for his voice."

"- His voice? You mean he had a bad voice?"

"I laughed and said: Well, a voice that had to be heard through an electrical thing definitely isn't a nice one." I explained chuckling slightly.

He raised his eyebrows and pressed on : "An electrical thing? Kindly explain a little more what you mean," leaning forward on his chair.

I am surprised when he says that; but I ignore my surprised and ask: "What do you mean by explaining? A disadvantaged throat is plain to see."

"-Do you mean to say that Mr. Shahi has no throat?" he now

"-Well, that was obvious. Even if his face was disfigured, you could see the breathing hole on his throat."

The major asks no more questions. He pauses a moment then gets up and simply says; Thank you."

He says goodbye and leaves. I wonder why Mr. Shahi's disadvantaged throat was so interesting and surprising to him. He couldn't have failed to see it? As far as I know all the body features of a victim are reported to the police by the coroner. Did they really miss it?

Sheila was due t to arrive soon. We had to do something but what? There was blood all over the floor and we couldn't dump Hassan Jighil's body anywhere. We wasted so much time and Sheila was there before we knew it. We were in a bad shape and she knew something was wrong. We made her understand what had happened. Leila explained everything to Sheila. But she didn't panic. She was calm and went to the kitchen and brought a knife and opened the door. We thought Hassan Jighil would jump on her any minute. She went inside. Leila called her sister. She asked: "Where are you, Sheila? What's happened?" "Say something". Sheila came out and said: "He's dead". As matter of   as if she were   a roach was dead. She didn't bat an eye and said she would help us get rid of the body.

I didn't go to her place anymore. I heard Leila say that every time her sister cut a piece of the body and dump it somewhere. Yes, that's how I turned into a murderer.

"- What a kind murderer."

-Arman, you were supposed to keep quiet.

Nazanin took the letter from Negar: "I read the rest of it."

I tell myself that I'd be happy to hear you reading it so I could see whether it was your voice I heard on the phone or not.

But I don't think that all killers must get punished. Do you think I must get punished? I did it for the sake of Leila and myself. I'm not sorry about what I did, Not only I'm not sorry, I feel satisfied that I have taken a rascal off the earth. I have sent this letter and ask you to publish it so every woman and girl can read it to know that it's not wrong to kill rascals of this kind. Other wises they would never have to pay for their crime. I am living my life. I'm very healthy. Although I have nightmares these nights, I am not sorry about what I have done. I killed in self-defense. To defend Leila. I'm writing this for the women who get raped and do nothing except beg and cry. They might say 'no, we couldn't do such a thing'. But a woman can always play a trick to get rid of these rascals even at the worst times.

Now I see why Sheila keeps being a prostitute though she is sick. She says she acts as bait for the men who cheat on their wives. I am a bait for dirty men. I don't want to be like her, but she's now the holiest prostitute I know. It's funny, isn't it? A prostitute that makes herself holy by what she does. I wish I could be in her shoes but I don't have the ingredients to be like her. But I wish I could really ruin all of these rascals.

Don't try to track me down. If I have done murder and I'm writing to you, this means I have planned everything. The address on this packet is a fake one. The names are also fictitious. Don't look for me and just have the courage to publish it.

"And you lack the courage to publish it, don't you?" I challenge.

-We do, but the magazine will be closed down if we do it.

-So, you don't have the courage. Then again I tell you, the way it's been made up, this letter is just a fictional story. Maybe, these things have happened but they must have happened in a different way. I find it hard to believe that they have actually butchered the dead body like that. I think it's a sheer lie.

-Why do you think that?

-Because it's been written by a murderer. While she's trying to hide he name and address, she's trying to hide the whole story too. She tells the story in a way that she cannot be traced. She's probably killed somebody but she's trying to make a hero of herself by telling the story like this.

"- That is only one possibility. You try to criticize it like a book."

-Yes, it's only one possibility, but I'm not saying that without any considerations. I think a while and then I say it. You too must consider this.

Nazanin says: Bravo, really, she's done a job, really.

-You're thinking like Arman too. On whose side are you, the murderer or the victim?

"-Come on, sister. The guy that was killed is a bastard. This could have happened to anybody. Let's think that this happened to me or you."

"-If it was so, we could talk to Arman or call the police."

"-No, sister. Our world is differ from theirs. They didn't have anybody. The girl who wrote the story was herself the black sheep of the family for Mastaneh and the other girl, Leila, didn't have any immediate family and lived with her sister who is prostitute and has AIDS. What would you do, if you were in her place? If you had nobody and everyone thought you were mean, wouldn't you try to do something to defend yourself?"

"-I wouldn't murder someone anyway."

"-Oh, you would." She replied matter of factly.

"-I wouldn't."

"-I say 'you would'. You would do it."

"Stop it."

Nazanin read the letter up to the part that we had already read and we read the rest of it together.

"-I'm still saying the same thing. The story hasn't been quite like that. This is now how things occurred but the events in this letter aren't too fictional"

I turn to Nazanin "Did any of your school or college friends have an abortion?"

"-There were several occasions like that." she nodded.

"-Excuse me, but aren't there any hookers in your college?"

Her face gets red and she says: " yes. There are also girls of this type and they do it to pay for college."

I turn to Negar "If I asked you to read the letter, it was only because of the murder that was committed and the narration that was like a story. Only this has made me a bit curious. I liked this girl because she had dared to defend herself. That's it. Even if she's a dreamer, it's pleasing to me. Do you understand? With a false address and a fake name, I believe she's killed someone. But not in the this way and maybe I'm wrong. When everything is a fake, nothing has to be a lie. But saying that she doesn't know, and Mastaneh hasn't told her how she got pregnant which is something I can't believe because they were close friends. Why she didn't say is anyone's guess."

Nazanin raises her hand, "I agree."

"-You're both of you nuts."

"-Don't make me open the door to let Mr. Shahi's ghost come for you." I tease.

"-Oh, you naughty boy. I had just forgotten it."

She goes to the kitchen while she's still nagging. Nazanin remains here "What did the policeman ask you?

"-Only asked the same questions he had asked me yesterday."

"-Well, why?"

"- I guess to see if there's any difference between what I say and now and what I said before."

"-I think they will come again. Wasn't anyone else involved with Mr. Shahi except you?" she continues.

-I might have to answer these questions again and again but I'm not scared because I haven't done it." I answer her.

"-Who do you think has murdered Mr. Shahi?"

I look at her for a few moments and say; "I just got rid of the Major and you're starting now. He had the same questions, but I had no answer to give him."

-Negar is anxious, says she's afraid, but she doesn't go on. "Afraid of what?" I ask. "That they might arrest me and take me for the one who did it? It is true that they think I am a suspect, but if they had any hard evidence, they would have arrested me yesterday. Not to mention, I wasn't home at that hour and I have a witness." Negar is now very anxious.

I tell myself that it's the right time to see if Nazanin has a hand in making that prank call or not. so I will ask her to repeat the 'hang up' for me, then and if her face changes and I will see that it was her and she will know I know about it. I turn to Nazanin, "Nazanin, I want you to repeat a sentence a couple of times. Just do it and don't ask why."

"-You want to play a game? What is it?"

"-Yes, you could say that. Just say 'Hang up', 'Hang up".

Without any changes in her voice she asks: "What that's it? You want me to say 'hang up' a couple of times?"

There is no change in her voice or her face.

"-Yes. Wouldn't you know? I just want you to say 'Hang up' a couple of times."

She shrugs and says "'Hang up'".

I close my eyes and listen to her voice carefully. Her voice is very much like the voice I had heard, but I cannot be sure. I don't have any convincing reason to accuse her either. Whatever the case, Nazanin holds no grudge against me or Negar, and even if she did, she wouldn't want to ruin her sister's life with a stupid move.

The three of us have dinner. It seems that Nazanin is still going to be our guest tonight. They go to the bedroom. I don't feel sleepy so I sit behind the computer. and check Shahi's weblog.

The last few days, I've been thinking all the time about Shahi, the prank call, and the familiar voice. I try not to talk to anyone about these things but it's useless.

I see he has a new post and I haven't read yet. I read it and I think it's the last message before his death, but when I check the date and hour of the post. I am really surprised. It's was posted only an hour ago! How can it be possible? Mr. Shahi is dead. I remember the dream that I had, where Mr. Shahi said 'you haven't seen the dead body". I remember the Major who was surprised when I said he had a hole in his throat. No way. I can't believe that he's alive and I can't also believe that someone else has posted this message. If Shahi is not dead then who was the dead body in her apartment?

"I'm still breathing. I'm still doing it. Thank god. I will keep writing as long as I breathe, maybe not on this weblog, maybe somewhere else to shout with my fake throat. I shout! I shout much deeper and louder than the silence of the night. I might as well go to the street and begin to play and make people laugh or cry like a dumb beggar. This is also a scream. Not always the sounds that we make form a 'scream'. It's sometimes a look, sometimes a fist and sometimes silence is a 'scream'. The thing is not to be calm before the injustice."

I am shaking. Can a ghost have a weblog post? I ask myself; "How do you know that Shahi himself has written this? Perhaps, it's done by the inspection team. They have done so to get a clue. It's easy for them to get the password." But they cannot write as he did, no matter how professional they are. These are all his words and sentences. I have read all his texts or perhaps I'm wrong when I think no one else can write in the same way. I want to leave him a message though I think it might be dangerous. Maybe her weblog is being controlled. Now, what am I going to say? But, the section where we could post our opinions is inactive. This makes me believe that Shahi has done it. If they wanted to trace anyone, they wouldn't do this. They would let others give their opinions to get hold of something.

I feel suddenly, someone behind me. I don't dare to turn around and see. The fear of what has happened has given me such illusion. The lights are off and there's only me and the light from the computer screen. I try to repeat to myself that there's no one behind me. I breathe heavily ,then, I turn sharply to look back. There's nothing except for my shadow reflected on the wall. I raise my hand and shake it to make sure it's my shadow. I turn back and read Shahi's text again and check the date and hour.

Now I am wet with sweat. It's one of those moments I don't know if I should laugh or cry. Now, why should I laugh or cry? I don't feel sleepy but my eyelids are heavy. I feel like doing something but what? At times like this, whatever you do, the police might treat you as a suspect. It's best not to do or say anything.

Once more, I feel someone is standing in the back of me, and I'm tired of it! I hear some sniffs and think it might be Negar, but I look back and I see no one. I stare into the darkness. In one corner of the room, I see somebody squatting like a shadow. She's sniffing and crying. Is it Nazanin or Negar? Why is she crying? Perhaps, it's Negar that is scared of Shahi's death and can't sleep. Whatever the case, she's a woman and things like that are not something to get over with. I want to turn on the lights.

"-No, don't. For god's sake." A voice pleads.

It's Nastaran's voice. I feel shaky again. I am afraid of going near her. I try to see her face in the dark, but I cannot see her. Her head is up and she looks at me.

"-What do you want coming here like a ghost? You stupid fool!" I chastise.

She looks down. She seems to have a handkerchief in her hands and wipes her tears with it.

"-I'm here to say goodbye."

"-Say goodbye?"

"-Yes. I'm going. I see now that you and I can't live together. Today, I wish you could say 'no, don't go' but you didn't say a word."

"-I never said it and won't say it," I affirm.

"-I know. Negar has come between you and me." she sniffle.s.

"-Yes. Negar is in your place. Not your place because it's hers anyway. You knew before that you no right to stay here. As long as Negar is here, with all the good and bad things about her, I don't want you to be with me. You get it?" I try to sound firm.

"-I get it very well."

"-I wish you had realized it earlier and had not bothered me so much. Now, why bother to say goodbye? You can leave without saying goodbye."

"-I'm going to leave here forever. I'm not coming back. I have just come here to say 'I love you' forever." She weeps.

"My heart is softening. I don't want to make her go away like I did before, but it seems she has decided go herself. Maybe that's her game for tonight. She gets up and comes a little close but I still can't see her properly yet.

"-Just tell me that you love me for the last time. That's all," she pleads.

"-I loved you. That's all."

She stands still for a new moments and then goes to the door. As she goes away, her shadow fades too and I cannot see her any longer. I stare at the direction in which she disappeared. I blame myself for keeping an imaginary being in my mind for such a long time, so she can annoy me any time she wants. I brought Nastaran in my mind and now I'm letting her out myself. I sit on the chair and lean my head against the back and close my eyes. I review all the days I spent with the imaginary and real Nastaran and ask myself "Did she really go away? For good?" I might miss her but I won't. how can I miss someone who's left me for another man? Apart from her beautiful mind, I also like her body that now in another man's arms. So, everything is finished, both the real and fictional 'Nastaran'.

Negar is now beside me and asks: "You're still awake."

I turn to look at her. Contrary to Nastaran's face, hers is quite visible.

"-Why aren't you sleeping?"

"-I couldn't. I don't know why."

But I do know why, and I know that she does too. The fear from Shahi's death is still in her head. She's a woman and there's nothing we can do. I have some fear too. I put a chair next to me and she sits on it. She puts her head on my shoulder and stares at the computer screen.

"-What are you looking for on the internet?"

"-I'm looking for you," I say tendency.

"-But I'm with you, why are you searching the internet to find me?"

I open the weblog in which I have posted our own photos. Since last year, I have been writing all my memories with her, and all the places that we have been to a and I have posted some photos of us too. But I had never told her that I have such a weblog. She can't believe it.

"-You naughty boy, since when did you started writing?"

I show her the date of my first post, it is the date of our marriage.

"-This is incredible! How could have the time to write anything that day. We had so much to do?" she asks astonished.

"-You must believe me. I wanted to show you someday and make you happy. Now, are you happy?"

"-I'm ecstatic. I can't believe you've written so much in one year and you haven't told me. You're so mean. Why did you keep this from me?"

"-I wanted to have something different for our wedding anniversary. This is my gift for this year."

She moves her neck to one side and asks: "Does this mean you won't buy me anything?"

I really wanted her to say 'What an awesome gift! This is worth more than everything else to me. I wanted her to say this is the best gift ever! I waited her to say....but does it really matter what I like?

Negar is not saying any of that and she just says that I'm so mean to keep this from her. Now she's asking if I'm not going to buy her anything this year.

I know that I must tell her that I will go and buy the one thing on her mind and think nothing of its price. But it's impossible to forget its price. Anyway, I say; "I will. How would you like the green manteaux?"

"She opens her arms, hugs me, kisses me, and exclaims: "What a lovely husband I have!"

Why am I a lovely husband whenever I want to buy her something? Why isn't it lovely that I'm living like a real human being?

"-Go and sleep." I command.

"-No, I want to stay with you."

"-Then, bring the mattress here, so we can sleep right here."

Negar brings the mattress. Nazanin has occupied our bed also.

Although I hate it when someone lies in my bed, I don't mention it to anybody. I don't have the energy to argue with anyone. I lie on the mattress. Negar lies besides me. I put a hand under her head and I put the other hand on her chest. It's dark but

Negar's eyes shine like that of a cat. She looks at me and says: "Why don't you go to sleep?"

I move closer to her, smell her hair, kiss her, and say: "I have had so much sleep today. Don't worry about me. You get some sleep and so will I."

She closes her eyes, but I'm thinking about Shahi, about Nastaran, about many things. I don't know what time it is or how long I have been thinking about the death of Shahi and Nastaran's departure. My eyelids are heavy, but I open them. In the dark room, I can see a man sitting on a chair right in front of me. I look sharp. It's the Major. How has he gotten in? He looks at me and says: "We know that you have killed Mr. Shahi."

"-Me? I haven't." I insist.

Suddenly Shahi puts the electric device to his throat and says: "Yes, he has. He has done it."

I shout; I haven't killed anybody! I haven't killed anybody!"

Then Seyyed says; "Yes, Major. It's him and I am a witness."

The janitor says; "I told you they would frame you after all."

Then Negar comes puts her arm round Seyyed, and laughs, saying: "Arman, I never cheated on you. Believe me."

Then Richard Gere says; "Don't believe it, you fool! Stupid idiot! Lunatic! Don't believe it. Your wife is just like mine."

Nastaran adds: "Now, you see? This is another witness. But you didn't take my word for it."

The small boy on the stone buffalo is ones again telling his mother: "Mom, this man here says that you have cheated on me because you said Uncle Pourang's Show has started."

The woman in the white dress enters and adds: His wife's has issues and thinks everyone is a cheater."

The taxi driver says; "Yes, pal. I want to find a wife for my son. Finding a wife for my son is no cheating, is it?"

Two girls who are wearing green manteaux chant: "Cheating, cheating!"

Then the girl with the story comes forward and declares: "I wrote that letter. I want to kill everyone and even you."

Babu says: "No, no, you must not die. Come. It will be cheap for you."

Amir the fruit-seller, who has his head bandaged hits him on the back of his head and says; "Shut up, you lousy bastard!"

Nazanin says: "Hang up. Hang up."

Soroush says: "I swear to God, what I do is not cheating; I only want to make real progress. Why do you think leaving the country is 'betrayal'?"

Seyyed who has now joined in says: "This filthy guy thinks I am cheating on people's beliefs."

"Shut up! All of you or I will.."

Seyyed then blows a whistle on me, as an almond-eyed man looks at me and says: "Forget it. Let's eat some embryo. Everything is Halal here."

The Major once again claims: "Now, we're absolutely certain that you have done Mr. Shahi."

"I haven't done it", I claim. I'm just a lunatic but I'm no murderer!"

Shahi interjects: We know that. If you weren't a lunatic, you wouldn't kill an important character like me."

The students from my class now are all standing before me and are shouting: "Insane! Insane! Insane!"

I begin to laugh as I'm also crying, as the Stone Buffalo attacks me.

"-Arman? Arman? Wake up! Arman! I'm telling you."

I open my eyes. Negar is scared. She's sitting beside me. I'm sweating all over. She looks directly at me.

"-You were having a dream. You were screaming."

She fetches me a glass of water.

"-Don't sleep. I'll make the breakfast."

The first thing that comes to my mind is Shahi's weblog. It's incredible, or perhaps I don't want to believe it. Whatever the case, this is my concern today. We have breakfast.

Negar says: "There's some noise coming from the outside."

"-It's the neighbors."

"-But we're on the last floor and Mr. Shahi is also..."

She stops. I pay more attention to the noises. It's from the outside. I don't finish my breakfast and go to the door. I open the door. The door to Mr. Shahi's apartment is open and some people are going in and coming out. They are not wearing police uniforms. Why aren't they wearing any uniforms? I step forward and take a look. Some people are busy collecting stuff. I set eyes on the Major. He looks at me. He walks straight to my side, his rather large body blocking me from seeing inside the apartment.

-Is something wrong?

-No, I just wanted to see what's up. I thought they were burglars.

No, they are not. It's us. You go to your apartment.

I sense anger in his voice as if he wants to get rid of me. I stare at him for a couple of moments to let him know that I'm not pleased with his tone of voice. Meanwhile, I see some people coming out of the apartment carrying a computer and some drawers. He steps to my side. I go to my own apartment and as I'm closing the door, I look at him again "I am curious to know if you saw the hole on Mr. Shahi's throat?"

He stares at me for a second and wants to make me understand that he doesn't like my question, then with a louder voice; "Please, go in."

I chuckle and close the door. Negar is pale "What's the matter?"

"-Nothing. It was the police."

"-I thought it was Mr. Shahi."

"-Why did you think like that?"

"-I don't know. I just had this thought."

"-Shahi is dead. Finish your breakfast," I command.

Suddenly I hear the doorbell. I'm angry that my breakfast is being interrupted again. I go and open the door. It's the Major "I want to warn you not to chase this case or you might suffer the consequences."

I look at him and say nothing. He doesn't say anything either. Maybe he wants me to say; "OK I won't chase anything." But this answer would be pleasing to him, so I don't say such a thing. I say: "His case or any other case doesn't concern me in the least. Aren't you the one responsible for it? I am a teacher. You do your job and I do mine."

I think he's going to punch me in the face with that large fist of his and sense the anger in his voice as he says; "I warn you anyway."

"-I expected to hear a kinder tone of voice for my cooperation with you."

He has not yet moved but I close the door anyway. I actually slam the door; I want to show him that I'm not scared of anything, that I'm minding my own business, that I don't like how he responded against my earlier judgment. Now, will he really get the message?"

I want to open the door and blow my whistle on him too, but you can't play with men of this profession. If I could do it right in front of him, I'm sure he would never forget it and I would pay for it forever. Suddenly my mind is occupied again: "Why weren't any of them wearing uniforms?"

I look at the clock. I must hurry not to be late. I have a few chunks and I am on my way. There's the bus, the crowd, and the school again. I go to the class. A student is on the watch outside the class. He goes in as soon as he sees me. There is no noise and everything looks fishy to me. I go in and say "Hi" but nobody answers. Nobody moves a muscle and Saberi is standing in front of the blackboard and saying nothing. stand and look at them without saying a word. I don't laugh but some of them want to laugh and are trying not to. I look at the blackboard. They have drawn a caricature of me. with a large head, small hands, tiny legs, and dragging a bag in his hand. his shirt is unfastened and his shoes are torn.

"I didn't know I'm so cute," I finally say.

The boys suddenly burst into laughter. Something falls over my head and makes a splash and small pieces of paper fall on my head. The boys stand to give me a clap. They congratulate me because it is Teacher's Day. I cannot hear my own voice amid all the noise. I try to calm them by giving them a hand signal .Finally they become quiet and I notice one of the boys is looking out. Seyyed is standing outside watching us through the half open door. He sets eyes on me and We exchange a momentary stare, then I close the door. The boys are saying funny things.

Saberi says; "Happy Teacher Day, sir!"

Ahmadi adds; "Happy Teacher Night too, sir!"

"Now, it is right for me to say that you must all go to hell." I   teasingly.

The boys laugh and I thank all of them.

 Then Saberi says; "We thought alot about what we could get for you, but, from what we know about you, you are a book lover so we ask everyone to bring a book for you."

They bring forward a carton with ribbons from the back and put it on the desk. I untie the gift and It's full of books. I am ecstatic to see them. Nothing could make me happier than this gift. "I thank you again. I hope you haven't gone through much trouble to get these books. You know that I am very frank. I say everything from the heart. You gave me the best gift."

The boys say "Hurray'" and give me a big hand. Once more I ask them to be quiet and say; "I have been given books before but I have never had so many."

Ahmadi speaks up: "Sir, everyone knew that you'd love to have books more than anything else."

Shakiba adds: "Is it all right if we talk about being a teacher and these stupid lessons that we hate today?"

- "No It's not all right. The bad thing is that there are eavesdroppers around here. What we talked about in the class was so easily passed on to the other teachers. And not to mention, we're coming to the end of the term and we cannot afford to lag behind. But we can do something else." I explain.

"What can we do, sir?"

"-This Friday, we can meet in Darakeh or Darband. Anyone who likes to join us is free to come and we can talk about anything you like."

I am going to buy the green manteaux. As I arrive at the square, I see a woman in a dirty dress who is begging for money and has tears streaming down her face. A little further on , there's a man with one leg who is stretching out his hand pleading: "Please, help me, for God's sake." A young girl wearing school uniform has a packet of chewing gum in her hand. She moves around in the crowd, pulling some sleeves, sayin: "Buy a chewing gum, please."

Some of the taxi drivers are exchanging swear words. A boy is rubbing his body against a girl who is looking in the shop windows. A motorcyclist is begging a police officer not to take his motorcycle away. A woman's leg has gotten stuck in a hole as she is walking on the bridge and the gives a painful cry. Beyond all these scenes, there is a woman crying out; "My bag, the thief got my bag!" And everyone is standing by watching the thief run away on a motorbike. The girl who is selling chewing gums now grabbing my sleeve, "Buy a chewing gum?"

I take out some money to give her. She checks the money, hands me two chewing gums, and smiles.I smile too. "No thanks. I don't want it. She frowns "You must have them."

" No, I'm not having them."

She puts the gums down on my shoes and says: "I'm no beggar, mister!"

The clouds suddenly cover the sun and it begins to rain. The people run to the sidewalk as a man saying to his wife; "Come here or you'll get wet."

But I stay in the rain to get wet, wet enough to let the rain fall all over my body. I just don't understand why people run away from the rain. Why does everybody tell the others to go under the rain when it rains like this?

I buy the green manteaux and have it wrapped up. As I'm walking in the rain I begin to think. Until now, all I had on my mind was finding the caller with the prank but I'm now letting it go. She didn't call anymore and I'm worried that it might lead to the familiar voice and then I might see a friend or someone I know and things might get somewhere I don't like them to get. But if she calls again, I won't stop until I have it settled down. I have no doubts about Negar. I wish she has the same feeling deep down. But what am I going to do about Shahi? I don't dare to follow the story anymore and there's nothing I can do about it. After reading his weblog messages and the date he had posted his messages, I believe that he's not dead, but if that is so, the cops didn't leave me alone so soon. Can it be that the weblog I have been visiting has nothing to do with Shahi? I had never seen him updating any posts. Perhaps it was someone else's weblog, someone with the same name 'Shahram Shahi" and he's been tricking me all this time to believe that the weblog is actually his. But how can I be sure that his name was really Shahram Shahi? But, no, the weblog goes with this title – "The Man With No Throat." How many web loggers do we have with no throat? If the weblog was actually his, then why didn't they investigate me anymore? Why did they ask me not to follow the story anymore? Or does he have anything to do with me?

As I'm coming to the alley, a police car goes by. Someone waves a hand to me from inside the car. I look sharp and see that Babu is back and is waving his handcuffed hands to me from inside the wet police car. I follow him with my eyes until the car vanishes. I get home, and as I am walking up the stairs, I remember Mr. Shahi. His robotic voice echoes in my head. I look at his door which has been sealed. I open the door to see that the curtains are drawn and the house is so dark. I'm surprised that Negar is not home yet. Suddenly I hear some voice from the sitting room and I feel worried. Who can it be? The fictional 'Nastaran' is no longer in my head. And Mr. Shahi is…. No, this voice is real. Who is that? I shout: "Negar! Negar!"

"-I'm here. Come."

I open the door to the sitting room. It's dark. All of a sudden, the lights are turned on and Negar burst into laughter. There's a small cake on the table. She comes to me and we kiss. She is wearing make-up and as neatly dressed.

"-First of all, Happy Birthday to you!" She hands me a pair of jeans with a light color and a big mark on its back and with two pockets on its sides. I try to show her that I'm happy but I'm not. Why do Nastaran and the kids from the school know what makes me happy and my wife has no idea? A pair of jeans, and this particular model, I have never worn any of these.

"-Do you like it?"

"-Yeah. I'm ecstatic." I lie

I recieve my gift. She jumps up and down and kisses me a couple of times. But I like to pick on her and grouch about the pants she has bought for me. "You do not know my taste after all we've been through?" I chide.

I am sure she would also say; "Are you insane? I have bought you a gift and this is how you thank me?"

But it's OK to keep it down this time; I shut up and say nothing. But the honor in my life is being insane: I'm insane when I make a stand against the stupid fools, against the people who cheat on beliefs, cheat on themselves and their wives and husbands. And I'm insane enough to grouch to myself and say "Idiot, where's your head. Behave yourself". I'm just too tired now. I am sick and tired of all the cries and groans for a little money that I have been hearing from the beggars on the street. I am sick of knowing that my friends are leaving to make a better life abroad. I am an exhausted lunatic.

I have had these sick feelings since I was a small child. The gum selling kids, a bunch of lousy mouths, stupid girls who fall for any boy, boys who only think about having fun with girls, girls like Mastaneh, Leila, Sheila and men like Jighil, Shahi and Babu.

So, I write all these things and I don't get offended if anyone calls me insane. Don't forget, I comb my hair back; I let a goatee grow on my chin and the sides of my face are cleanly shaved; I wear a suit and I hold a Papco case. Anytime I see someone who's acting weird or talking weird or saying the F word, I stare into their eyes and say; "Idiot! Stupid! Fool!"

If you ever see anyone with these features, don't have any doubts that it's me and you can make fun of me as much as you like and you may call me "Insane! Insane!"

The End

One day, while I was writing this story, my wife asked; "Once your book is published, would you say on the first page of the book that you're dedicating it to your wife?"

I replied: "I don't have this childish attitude. I am not writing it for you, so why would I do that? The book is first for me, and then for the readers."

She was upset, but didn't say a thing. Then, I thought about why writers dedicate their works to someone. At that time, I realized that I had spent a long time with a pencil in my hand as I was writing the story, and my wife was behind me; and she was getting along with me patiently.

There were many days when she played with our baby boy to let me go on without any disturbance. It was then that, I set my mind on dedicating my book to my wife, because if she hadn't been there for me, the book would never have been finished. But also I am a bull-headed guy, and I always keep my word, I do not dedicate the book to my wife on the first page; I am doing it on the last page.

But I write it, anyway:

Dedicated to my wife. With love and respect.

And I would like to express my gratitude to Mrs. Samira Yekehbash, Mrs. Mahnaz Badihian, Mrs. Dorothy Payne, Mr. Ibrahim Daryaei Motlagh and the other friends who helped me improve the book with their honest words.